Flower Moon

ALSO BY GINA LINKO
Flutter
Indigo

GINA LINKO

Sky Pony Press
New York

Sky Pony Press books may be purchased in bulk at special discounts for sales promotion, corporate gifts, fund-raising, or educational purposes. Special editions can also be created to specifications. For details, contact the Special Sales Department, Sky Pony Press, 307 West 36th Street, 11th Floor, New York, NY 10018 or info@ skyhorsepublishing.com.

Sky Pony® is a registered trademark of Skyhorse Publishing, Inc.®, a Delaware corporation.

Visit our website at www.skyponypress.com.

10 9 8 7 6 5 4 3 2 1

The Library of Congress has cataloged this book as follows:
Names: Linko, G. J., author.
Title: Flower Moon / Gina Linko.
Description: New York : Skyhorse Publishing, [2018] | Summary: Tempest and Tally Temple, mirror twins inseparable since birth, are now thirteen and being pulled apart by the same force that has separated other twins in their family, but Tally is determined to fight back.
Identifiers: LCCN 2017031374 (print) | LCCN 2017043624 (ebook) | ISBN 9781510722750 (eb) | ISBN 9781510722743 (hardcover : alk. paper) | ISBN 9781510722750 (ebook)
Subjects: | CYAC: Sisters--Fiction. | Twins--Fiction. | Individuality--Fiction. | Supernatural--Fiction. | Magnetism--Fiction. | Carnivals--Fiction. | Family life--Fiction.
Classification: LCC PZ7.L66288 (ebook) | LCC PZ7.L66288 Flo 2018 (print) | DDC [Fic]--dc23

Cover design by Sammy Yuen
Cover illustration by Manuel Šumberac

Printed in the United States of America

For Zoe, Maia, Jack,
and, of course, for you.

Flower Moon

1

Seeing as it was the last day before summer break, the other sixth-grade classes were doing stuff that made sense: signing each other's yearbooks, playing hangman on the whiteboards, or participating in the student-teacher field day on the front lawn.

But not Mr. Umberto's class—my class. No, we were in the science lab, watching my twin sister pass out eight-by-ten laminated copies of Mr. Umberto's school photo, while the hooting and hollering of the kickball games outside floated in through the lab's open windows.

Tempest had persuaded Mr. Umberto to let her do another science presentation in front of the class, even though the last one hadn't gone so well (let's just say that near-electrocution isn't exactly smiled upon in a middle-school science lab).

"Yes, we get to draw mustaches on Mr. Umberto," Tempest said as she started passing out magnets. "Tally helped me prepare these photos last night, and if you look beneath the plastic covers, there should be a bunch of fuzzy-looking, black pieces of iron floating around."

Tempest held up a photo of our bald and way-too-smiley teacher. "Watch." She raised the magnet in her hand and began to drag the iron filings into place, "drawing" hair on top of the glare coming off Mr. Umberto's bald head.

Tempest waited for a reaction. To everyone else, I'm sure she looked like normal, everyday Tempest, but I saw the tension in her face, the stiff way she held her shoulders, her too-frequent blinks. She usually liked to stay behind the scenes, so this was a big deal to her. This was Tempest being brave.

Bradley Ballard balled up his copy of the photo and chucked it toward the wastebasket. "We're not six years old," he groused as he leaned back on his rear chair legs.

Bradley Ballard. I hated that kid. He was onions and anchovies. He was a spider floating dead in the bottom of your thermos.

"Leave Tempest alone," I hissed at him.

I mean, he was right, kind of. We weren't six. But, holy green beans, did I want to stick my foot out and hook it around the back leg of his chair. Just give it a good yank. And watch him fall ears over elbows onto his head. Oh, how satisfying it would be.

My foot twitched. I watched Tempest blink several times, holding one blink a blip too long. She swallowed hard, and my throat pinched.

I very much needed this experiment to go okay for her.

"I remember having a toy like this when I was little," Marisol Phillips said. With a giggle, she gave an iron-filing Mohawk to her own Mr. Umberto, and the kids near her responded with a chorus of laughter.

Thank you, Marisol.

After that the class got real busy giving Mr. Umberto some much-needed hair. We snickered at the different creations: fuzzy Elvis sideburns, an enormous lumberjack beard, a sleek comb-over.

"I have my hair back!" Mr. Umberto joked. "It's a follicular miracle."

Tempest chuckled and continued her presentation. "Magnets attract and repel. What's happening here is that the magnets are attracting the iron in the filings. But, you know, magnets are powerful. Magnetic fields are everywhere around us. Even inside us. The heart is the strongest electromagnetic field in the body."

She paused here, and I could tell it was practiced, for maximum effect. Then she continued, her voice animated, everything about her screaming enthusiasm.

It made me think of Pa Charlie's—our grandpa's—old, antique Philco. It was a console radio from the 1940s, bigger than a kitchen stove and encased entirely in gleaming, polished wood. One day, a couple of years ago, out back in our garage, Pa Charlie pulled out its innards. Wires and tubes and coiled pieces of metal were strewn across the garage floor. It looked like nothing but a mess to me, it really did. But Tempest had sidled right up to Pa Charlie. "What are these things?" she'd asked. And Pa Charlie sat down on the floor, his half-moon glasses down on the end of his nose, and explained each piece to Tempest and me.

Capacitors and resistors, volts and frequencies. Circuits, amplifiers, transistors. Tempest's eyes had lit up with each new word. She loved all kinds of mechanical stuff: taking apart Dad's old pocket watch, copying blueprints for a combustion engine from a library book, that kind of thing. But after that day with the radio, she became obsessed—even if, to me, it was all about as interesting as mothballs.

Pretty soon after, Tempest started inventing things: a home-made hearing aid for our neighbor; a solar heater for Bones's doghouse; a motorized mouse for our old cat, Mary Anning, to chase.

Those inventions made me awful proud of Tempest.

But that day, with the radio—when I looked back on it, it made me sad too.

It was maybe the first time I noticed it. Any serious differ-ence between my sister and me.

Watching Tempest's magnet demonstration, I suddenly missed my twin something fierce. A sharp pang filled up that space under my ribs—my breadbasket, as Pa Charlie would call it. I missed the Tempest who hadn't yet decided she had better things to do than to *be with me*, graffitiing the neighborhood sidewalks with chalk art, digging for fossils out in our back field, nursing our latest stray skunk or puppy or disgusting crayfish back to health.

We used to be inseparable: me coming up with the schemes, Tempest following my lead, my always-faithful partner.

I missed that.

In the Trenton Sisters Mystery books I read, neither of the sisters went off and *did her own thing.*

I watched Tempest put on her enormous green safety goggles. She clasped her hands under her chin all excited-like, the goggles making her pigtails stick out at odd angles. "Fellow sixth graders, how would you like to levitate a frog?"

I felt the tips of my ears burn then, embarrassed at how dorky Tempest sounded, and all my sadness vanished, just like that. I knew it made me a snot. But we were almost thirteen, for creamed corn's sake. Did she have to say things like "Fellow sixth graders"? And the pigtails, when was she going to give those up?

Tempest produced a glass jar from one of the cabinets and pulled something out of it. "Tally, come here. Hold this," she said, shoving her closed hands toward me.

I got up from my desk. "Is it the frog?"

"Of course!" Tempest answered, handing it to me. The frog felt slimy and alive, its heartbeat quick and even against my palm.

"Isn't he going to mind being levitated?"

"It's a she, and I don't think so. But I haven't asked her." Tempest smiled to herself as she continued with her setup. On the lab table in front of her sat all the bits and bobs of her experiment: tangles of copper wiring; a glass jar filled with green liquid; several sizes of batteries; and two large, super-strong electromagnets that Tempest had gotten special permission to use.

And of course the wriggling, slimy amphibian in my hands.

"Do frogs have ears?" I asked.

"Sorta. The circles behind their eyes, they're called tympanum." She clamped one of the wires to a small battery, then the other end of it to the electromagnet. I felt a hum—a strange pulsing vibration—thrum to life around me. It prickled at my skin, setting my teeth on edge.

I looked at Tempest, and her eyes met mine for only a second, her brow knit.

Just then, the frog started in my hands, and she jumped from my grasp, landing on the floor with a dull thud.

"Get her!" Tempest said.

"Yeah, Tally. Hop to it," Bradley teased.

"You girls need, um, help?" Mr. Umberto asked. He glanced at the clock, looking nervous. We had ten minutes left before the bell. Mr. Umberto was probably sorry he had ever agreed to this.

I bent down on my knees and reached for the tiny green booger of a frog, but she slipped out of my hands. I lunged after her, knocking into a couple of kids' legs and their desks, until finally I caught her.

All the while, that weird buzz shifted and surged around me. Growing.

It actually pushed me back on my heels for a second, and I struggled to catch a breath. It was like my asthma was acting up, almost exactly. After a minute, the air seemed to steady itself, the whirl and hum settling into more of a purr. But I still felt it take root right inside my throat, my eardrums, even my back teeth.

I stood up and looked out at the audience of kids in my classroom. Weren't any of them feeling this?

But, no, it didn't seem like it.

"Come here," Tempest said. She messed with a few more things on the table, and then she clamped another wire to a super-big battery, one that looked like it belonged under the hood of a car. The moment the prongs of the clamp hit the battery, it sparked something inside and around me. The thrum of energy kicked up a notch. I staggered backward a step.

Tempest watched me closely, her tongue sticking out through the corner of her lips like it always did when she was in deep concentration. But then she looked away.

Mr. Umberto checked the clock again. "Tempest, how exactly are you going to accomplish this levitation? And can I help?"

"We're nearly ready. And it's magnets, sir. If you get a powerful enough magnetic field, it acts on the frog's electromagnetic charges—specifically, all the water inside its body. We could use mice too, but frogs are better. Tally?" She turned to me.

I took a step toward Tempest and her equipment, but the air pushed back at me something fierce.

I took another step, and the closer I got to Tempest's equipment, the stronger the atmosphere pushed against me. My teeth were darn near chattering with the vibration of it all.

A sharp bolt of fear sizzled right down my spine.

I mean, how much of a warning did a girl need? Tempest was about to blow this place up or set the whole lab on fire—and humiliate herself in the process. I couldn't let her go ahead with whatever this was. I had to do something.

Anything.

I made a decision then.

I took a step closer, feigning like I was handing over that slippery frog. But I fixed my feet just right, and I forced myself to trip over the extension cord running across the front of the room.

I really gave in to the drama of it, made a right production of things—flailed my arms, yelped out loud, the whole shebang.

The frog flew from my grasp, and I purposely tangled my foot in the cord and kicked hard, making sure to yank it out of the wall. On my way down to the floor, I swiped an arm across the lab table in front of me, bringing bits of equipment down with me. A battery, a knot of wires, and the beaker full of iron filings came crashing down with me, onto the classroom floor, with a disastrous clatter and clank. The class erupted in laughter.

I groaned dramatically and turned onto my back, pulling in a huge breath. Relief. The pulsing nastiness was gone.

But then I saw a pile of Tempest's papers hanging over the edge of the desk. As I watched, the top one smoldered, then sparked and crackled. Somehow it caught true fire, a great flame leaping from the desk.

Chaos. Commotion. The whole class yelping.

"Okay, okay, kids. Calmly make your way outside," Mr. Umberto said, snapping at the flame with a dish towel. I was nearly trampled by my classmates as he smothered the fire and wiped at his forehead. "Miss Trimble, are you okay?" he asked.

"I'm fine!" I called.

"I was asking your sister," he said, looking down at me with something like exasperation.

I sat up, brushing iron filings from my forehead, and looked for Tempest. Her eyes met mine as she handed Mr. Umberto the fire extinguisher.

Her stare was hard. She knew.

I stood up. "I—"

"I'll get the shop vac," Tempest said, and turned and stalked to the door.

Mr. Umberto eyed me over the stream of the fire extinguisher.

"What?" I asked him.

"You did that on purpose."

"What? Why—Who would—" I sputtered.

"She worked very hard on this, Tally Jo, and was very much looking forward to it. She had it all under control."

I was irked now. "She did not have it under control!" Hadn't he felt what was in the air? What Tempest herself had started? "I was just saving her from—you know—like last time."

Mr. Umberto gave me a weary look. He shook his head and set down the fire extinguisher. "I'm going to go find Tempest. You, Tally, have a good summer. Okay?"

"I was saving her," I repeated.

He turned back with a sigh. "Were you saving *her*, or were you saving *you*?"

I had some weird pang in my breadbasket again, and suddenly I couldn't meet Mr. Umberto's gaze. My eyes searched the floor for that darn wayward frog. "You want me to help clean up, or . . ."

"No. I'm sure your sister will clean up with me when she gets back with the shop vac."

I nodded, feeling a lump of something curious and uncomfortable in my throat.

Then I left.

I kicked my heels around in the gravel of the playground, the early June sun burning down on the back of my neck, while the rest of my class milled around signing yearbooks and chattering excitedly about the fire. Tempest and Mr. Umberto were still inside.

"You okay?" Marisol asked, touching me lightly on the elbow.

"Yeah."

"What happened in there?"

Suddenly, I was irritated. "What do you think happened? Tempest and her ideas."

Mr. Umberto came through the doors just as the exit bell rang. "Everything's fine now, kids. Fire's out. You can come back in if you need anything. But, if not, enjoy your summer vacation!" His words were swallowed up in the swarm of kids racing out the school doors, hooting and hollering.

I watched the crowd, but I didn't see Tempest.

"You should take it easier on her," Marisol said, following my gaze. "Here." She shoved my yearbook at me. "I grabbed it on the way out."

"Thanks." I followed Marisol toward the crosswalk, joining a knot of kids from our class.

"Can I sign your yearbook?" Seth Bowers asked when he saw me, and he took the book from my hands.

Bradley Ballard walked past with his usual posse, tossing something back and forth with his friend Evan. It took me a minute to realize it was Tempest's frog.

"That really dills my pickle," I grumbled and stomped over to Bradley. "Give it here."

"No." He smirked, tossing the frog high in the air. The frog flailed and flipped. My temper flared.

"Give me the darn frog, or I'm going to—"

"What? You gonna go tattle to Mr. Umberto? Or why don't you go get your bonkers sister so she can fry us with one of her inventions?" He cackled. "And by the way, Tally Trimble, you know it was me who messed up her last little science thingy last time. We turned up the knob on that doohickey so it would go *ka-blam*."

"You worm." My fists balled at my sides.

Evan threw the frog into the air again, but I pushed Bradley out of the way and caught her, barely, grabbing just the ends of her skinny little legs. This poor frog. What a day.

"Go ahead, keep the thing," Bradley spat. "Maybe your sister can kill it later and you can eat frog legs for dinner."

"Shut up, Bradley. You leave my sister alone. You hear me?"

"Why? You don't even like your sister, her stupid pockets full of batteries and wires and nerdy garbage. You hate her moronic inventions and that stupid smile on her face even when everyone's making fun of her." He took a step closer to me and hissed, "I see how annoyed you get with her, Tally. You want to sock her yourself."

"Shut up, Bradley!"

"Tally, you know I'm telling the truth." He laughed again.

I handed the frog to Marisol, who took her with a squeak. Seth looked back and forth between us.

I closed the space between Bradley and me, and I poked him hard once in the chest. "You shut your mouth right now, or I will shut it for you."

"Tally," Seth said, touching my elbow, but I yanked it away.

Bradley smirked. "And what if I don't?"

I was so close I could see the dandruff in his hair, the little pimples above his lip, and I caught a whiff of his breath: always and forever smelling like onions.

He narrowed his eyes, daring me. "Your sister is nothing but a stupid moron."

Everything went red. Everything except the greasy shimmer of sweat on Bradley's upper lip. It felt like when my asthma kicked in and I couldn't breathe, and everything focused down into a point. Air, it was all I needed then. One thought. One goal.

Except now, looking at Bradley, all I could see was that sneer. One thought. One goal.

I balled my hand into a fist. I cocked my arm back, ready to knock his teeth in. God, it was going to feel so good.

But something slowed me down. Something pressed in on my brain. This weird pressure on my skull, nagging, niggling. It made me pause.

And I could not throw that punch.

I *wanted* to punch Bradley Ballard. I *needed* to punch Bradley Ballard.

But all of a sudden, I couldn't let go. Was it my conscience?

Whatever it was, I *couldn't* throw that punch. And, holy granola, I wanted to.

"You chicken or something?" Bradley said, right up in my face. I wiped his spittle from my forehead with the back of my hand, and I struggled for a deep breath, hearing that asthma-whistle in my chest.

Then I reached out, cool as a pickled cucumber. And I flicked him on his forehead.

Just my middle finger and my thumb, right there. *Flick.* Dismissing him. And it made such a sharp little sound.

It kind of took me by surprise, so I laughed. And that was more than Bradley Ballard could take. He pushed me, both hands on my shoulders, shoving me hard. I fell backward onto the asphalt and landed, with a thud, on my butt.

I scrambled to get up, but Bradley and Evan were already taking off, running away like the cowards they were. Mr. Umberto's voice rang out from behind me. "What's going on out here?"

"Nothing," I heard Marisol respond sweetly. "You want a frog?"

"Tally, you all right?" Mr. Umberto asked.

"Yes sir," I said, taking the hand Seth Bowers was holding out and pulling myself up.

"Those boys giving you trouble?" Mr. Umberto asked.

"Don't worry about it, sir," I said. "You have to pick your battles. Plus, it's summer now."

Mr. Umberto let out a low question of a laugh, and he turned back to Marisol. "Yes, I will take that frog. Tempest is going to show me how the thing was supposed to go." He took the frog and headed toward the school. "You got yourself one genius of a sister, Tally," he called over his shoulder.

"Yes sir," I said.

As Marisol and Seth started toward home, I paused to look toward the steps of the school.

I knew she was there. I could feel it.

Tempest stood at the open door, waiting for Mr. Umberto. She looked right at me, her round owl eyes boring into me. She was angry. No, furious. Had she seen the whole exchange?

"She'll get over it," Marisol said, seeing my focus on Tempest.

"Get over what?" I said, rolling my eyes. I fell into step with her, walking toward the corner.

"You know, how you always . . . like—" Seth stammered, and then he caught my eye. "Nothing. I don't know what I'm talking about." He smiled at me. "Flicking his head, Tally. That was a great move."

"Yeah." I grinned without meaning to.

Marisol look at me and then, her voice quiet, said, "For a second there, I thought you were going to punch him."

"So did I," I answered. And I realized something then. Something big. Something forceful. Something scary.

I stopped walking, dead in my tracks.

Could it have been Tempest?

Had Tempest somehow stopped me from clocking Bradley Ballard?

But I didn't really need to ponder that question—because I knew it was true. I knew it suddenly, in a bone-deep way, the question answering itself as soon as it formed.

I turned around and looked back at the school.

Tempest was in there. Inside the building, doing whatever she was doing with that frog and a heap of oversized magnets. I could feel her there. Existing.

I always could.

I quickly turned on my heel, away from our usual route home, and I started to jog.

"Where are you off to now, Tally?" Marisol called.

"I need to be somewhere," I called back.

"But I have your yearbook," Seth said.

"I'll get it later."

"You better not be chasing after Bradley," Marisol called.

I didn't answer her, but that wasn't where I was going. I didn't care about that anymore.

But Tempest pressing on my brain somehow, influencing me, keeping me from throwing that punch . . .

That mind trick was another story.

2

Much later, I trudged up the back steps of my house, sweaty and worn out from cleaning the kennels and playing with the dogs at Pleasant Paws Animal Shelter. It wasn't my usual volunteer day, but Dr. Francimore didn't mind when I just stopped in.

Sometimes animals were so . . . easy. Especially when humans weren't.

I opened my screen door, and Bones came bounding out of nowhere. I bent to greet him, petting his withers. He sat down like a good mutt and nuzzled my knees with his shaggy brown muzzle, his tail beating a happy rhythm against the wood floor. "I missed you too, boy."

I rubbed his belly and listened to the indistinct rise and fall of my parents' voices from the dining room. I couldn't hear my sister, but I knew she was with them.

I felt her there.

Growing up, we could never play hide-and-go-seek. Because of the pull.

It's what we had between us. That's how I always thought of it: *the pull.*

It was an invisible tether, pulling at my sternum and pointing me toward my sister, wherever she was. We could never truly play hide-and-go-seek because we always found each other, first stop. No question. It was a weird thing, I guess, if you took time to look it in the eye. But I tried not to.

Had she really stopped me from punching Bradley? Was it such a stretch to think that Tempest could've weaseled her way inside my very own brain?

Twins shared everything. But this . . . *this.* My decisions were supposed to be my own. Weren't they?

Because, doggone it, Bradley Ballard deserved a good punching. I pictured his sweaty lip again, and I felt a new swell of anger at my sister for stopping me.

Along with something else: amazement.

How did she do it?

When I was little, I believed in magic. All kinds of it. Wishes on shooting stars. Yanking on the wishbone. Reading people's minds. Truly, someday I expected to figure out how to converse with every animal on the planet, if I could just listen correctly.

Did I still believe in magic?

Then I had a scary thought: *I bet that wasn't the first time Tempest poked her way into my brain.*

A couple of weeks ago I had scraped up a heaping pile of Bones's poop into a paper bag, and I was just about to light it on fire on Evan's front porch. But I couldn't go through with it. Which was very unlike me.

And then, a few Sundays ago, I very nearly ripped Father Tom's toupee off his head while he was giving us the sacrament. Actually, on second thought, I was very glad Tempest had stopped me from going through with that one. Mama might never have recovered.

But wasn't Tempest breaking some kind of unwritten code of twin conduct?

How was she doing it? And *why*?

"Tally Jo, dinner!" Dad called.

"Coming!" I stood up and let Bones out into the backyard.

I walked into the dining room and took my seat, all the while pinning my laser-beam eyes onto my sister, telling her with my stare, *I know it was you. Inside my brain, bamboozling me into good behavior.* But she didn't look up. Instead she made out like she was oh-so-busy buttering a biscuit.

Mama said, "Tempest told us what happened at school today."

"Did she, now?"

"Don't sass your mother," Daddy warned.

"Yes sir," I answered, as Mama heaped a generous portion of rice on my plate. "Thank you," I muttered and unfolded my napkin.

Mama sighed.

I poured myself a glass of milk, waiting. I knew it was coming.

"So, what do you have to say for yourself?" Mama asked.

Wide-eyed and feigning innocence, I asked, "And exactly what events would you be referring to?"

"Tally," Daddy said.

"You ruined my entire science experiment today on purpose," Tempest blurted without looking up from her plate.

"I did not ruin it," I said. "I saved you from a disaster."

Mama's and Daddy's eyes were sharply trained on me. "What disaster?" Daddy asked.

I opened my mouth to answer, but Tempest interrupted. "The disaster of embarrassing my sister." And Tempest looked at me then, her eyes so full of something . . . not anger exactly.

"That's not true! You can't tell me you didn't know that—your equipment was about to—you know—*kaboom!*"

"It was not," Tempest said, but without a lot of conviction.

So I pounced. "I mean, the equipment did start an actual fire, Tempest. Let's not forget that small detail."

"A fire?" Mama cut in. She put down her fork and knife. "You didn't say anything about a fire, Tempest."

"It was nothing. Just a spark," Tempest answered, waving it away with her hand. "After the kids left and we were done with the fire extinguisher, I got the frog to levitate, Dad. It floated right in the air!"

"A fire extinguisher? Tempest!" Mama scolded, just as Dad slapped his hand on the table.

"You did it?" Dad asked. "It worked?" Tempest and Daddy exchanged a smile.

"No one got hurt?" Mama asked.

"That little flame was nothing," Tempest said.

"I hardly think a fire at school is nothing," Mama said.

Tempest sighed. "Tally nearly came to blows with Bradley Ballard though." Of course she'd diverted the attention to me. A classic move.

"Tally." Mama pursed her lips, her shoulders falling. "Again?"

"I *nearly* did, but I didn't. And he deserved it." I turned toward my sister. "But *somehow* I couldn't go through with it." I worked my eyeballs like laser beams again, trying to get Tempest to answer me, but suddenly she was all too interested in her country-fried steak.

Mama said, "Tally, do we need to have another conversation about controlling your temper?"

Tempest had set a fire in our science lab, but instead we were going to talk about my temper? The injustice of this family.

"No, ma'am," I grumbled. A few years ago, when I protected my sister from other kids and their teasing, I was the hero, and now . . . I was some kind of enemy. It didn't make a whole heap of sense.

"Tally Jo," Mama said, "you're nearly thirteen. You've *got* to start—"

"Thinking first, before I act. I get it, Mama. I do. And I didn't punch him! I flicked him." I demonstrated, flicking my fingers toward my father. "That's it."

"A flick, huh?" Daddy shrugged and looked at Mama, a smile playing around his lips. "Shows some emotional restraint, don't you think, Genevieve? Better than a kick in the ribs."

Mama rolled her eyes. "Really, William? I don't think—"

Tempest interrupted then, her voice quiet. "Bradley Ballard did deserve it, Mom. He really did." Tempest looked up at me and she gave me a nod.

There was my sister. The one I knew.

My sister: well-oiled gears, a cricket singing at night, quiet and hidden. Me: a match itching to be struck, motion and noise, edges prickly like a pinecone.

Mama sighed and took a bite of her steak. She cleared her throat and said, "Your father and I want to talk to you about this summer."

Something in my chest tightened right up. This had to be big if Mama was going to quit with her lecture and move on to something else. I looked over at Tempest. Our eyes locked and she shrugged. After too many beats of silence, I blurted, "Well, what in the pork 'n' beans is it?"

Daddy answered, "You two girls get to go to Pa Charlie's this summer on your own."

"You mean, without y'all?" Tempest asked, her brow furrowed.

"Why?" I asked at the same time.

"Because you'll have fun," Mama said.

Daddy added, "It'll be an adventure."

"What in the world are y'all going to do without us?" I asked, blowing at my hair to keep it out of my eyes. No matter how many times I redid my ponytail, there were always a million flyaway hairs 'round my face.

"We'll manage," Daddy said.

We sat in silence for a few moments, all of us listening to Bones's eternal scratching at the screen door. I studied my parents' faces: Mama's lifted eyebrows, Daddy's rigid smile.

Tempest broke the silence. "Tally's going to want to bring the dog."

"Can I, please?"

Mama shook her head.

"Why aren't y'all coming?" I asked. "I mean, that's why you're teachers though, so we can always travel with Peachtree Carnival in the summers."

"We have a lot to do around here," Daddy answered. "Your mother is going to work on her sculptures, and I'm finally going to finish remodeling the attic so you two can have your own rooms."

I said, "We don't need our own—"

"Can I have the one in the attic?" Tempest interrupted.

I blinked and looked over at my sister. She was excited about separate rooms? Of course she was.

"We'll have to discuss who goes where. But surely you'll both want your own room come the teen years," Mama said. Like it was so very important in that moment.

Suddenly, I didn't like this one bit.

Something was going on. More than they were saying.

"You'll have each other at the carnival," Mama said. "And we'll meet up with y'all near your birthday. It's not like we're abandoning you for the whole summer. Just a couple weeks."

"There's no other reason you want rid of us?" I tried one more time.

Tempest piped up, all forced cheerfulness. "It'll be great, I think. Won't it, Tally?"

I looked over at Mama. And, just for a second then, I saw something flash over her face. That Sad Mama look: her far-away eyes, the look I always hated.

Mama: a beautiful egret in regal stance, a window seat to cuddle into and sit reading, a secret wrapped in silk.

"Fine," I said. "Even though you won't tell us what in the jelly donut is really going on. I guess we can handle a few parentless weeks. Me and Tempest'll find some trouble to get into."

"Tempest and I," Mama corrected. Her fork shook a little when she went to chase after a bit of rice at the edge of her plate. What was with all this mystery? I wanted to ask what was really going on.

But something inside me let all the questions go.

I shot a glance at Tempest. Was she somehow forcing me to let this conversation drop? Needling into my brain?

I watched Tempest take a long swig of milk, listened as my parents' silverware hit their ivy-bordered china plates, and sighed.

No. This was just me shutting up for once.

"It'll be fun. Like we're all grown up," Tempest whispered that night from her bed, as I lay in mine, reading my latest Trenton Sisters Mystery.

"The carnival?"

"Yep."

I considered this. "Yeah," I said, turning my head so I could see her profile in the soft light, her blonde hair framing her face in a halo. "You don't think something strange is going on with Mama and Daddy?"

"Probably," Tempest said. The way she said it, sort of unconcerned and superior, it got under my skin.

"What do you know?" I sat up and shut my book.

"Nothing," she said, pulling the covers up to her chin, reaching over and shutting off the lamp between our beds. "I don't know anything."

"You do too," I said.

Tempest sighed. "I know that Mama and Daddy don't want to tell us more. Something probably is going on, but . . . we'll find out what it is when they want us to."

"Could Mama be having a baby or something?"

"Nah, they're too old. Don't you think?"

"Are they arguing? Getting divorced?"

"I don't think it's anything like that, Tally. It could be something totally cool. Maybe it's a surprise for our birthday."

"Our golden birthday." I smiled.

"Thirteen's a good number." I could hear the matching smile in her voice. "Don't worry so much. It'll be good to see Pa Charlie though. Everybody. Digger." Tempest yawned loudly.

"Yeah." I thought about Digger and his pristine comic book collection, the gap between his teeth, the way he could never outrun me, even on his best days. "Think he'll still want us to sneak the poor kids onto the rides for free?"

"If he's still Digger."

I lay back, snuggled into my blankets. Digger had a great laugh, like a car engine just starting to rev up. "Hey, Tempest."

"Hmm?"

"How did you do it?"

"What?" And I could tell in her voice, even in that one word, she knew.

"I know it was you. Earlier. When I was trying to punch Bradley."

"You didn't really want to hit Bradley."

"Yes, I did."

"Did you, *really*, Tally?"

"Tempest, you're not answering my question. How did you do it?"

"Tally, I'm trying to sleep already."

She turned away from me, onto her left side, like she always did when she was falling asleep, and I let it go. I listened to her breathing, and after a while it became slow and regular.

Then, like the many hundreds of nights before, I waited for a few moments, wondering at that feeling of being truly alone.

I liked it and I didn't.

I tried to summon all my mental powers and laser beam them over to Tempest. Force her to throw the blankets off and sit up to talk to me like she used to. Have her come over into my bed, snuggle right next to me, face-to-face, and talk till Mama and Daddy would yell at us to just, "Go to bed already!"

Nothing happened though. Nothing at all. She didn't obey my mind powers. She didn't even twitch.

How had she done it earlier, with Bradley Ballard?

And how in the world did *she* get to have this power over *me*? I mean, if anybody was going to discover a secret super-power like that, surely it was supposed to be me. I was the leader, wasn't I?

I was the bold one, the brave one. How many times had I come to Tempest's rescue? On the playground, in the lunch-room. Heck, just a few weeks ago, I'd dressed up in a pair of her cargo shorts and her favorite roller-skate tank top—plus the pigtails, of course—and pretended to be her so I could per-form her part in a group-project-turned-song-and-dance about the Bill of Rights in Ms. Schwartz's history class. Seemed Tempest could only locate her bravery for science things.

But I didn't mind. Usually. That's how we worked. Tempest liked to keep to herself. I dealt with the worst of things, shel-tered her from the world when necessary.

Mama liked to say that I was born kicking and screaming, looking for a fight, and Tempest was born wide-eyed and
silent, looking for me.

I stared up at the ceiling of our bedroom, at all of our glow-
in-the-dark stars shining a yellowy-white. The soft purple light
of the moon shimmered through our curtains.

I turned onto my right side, curled up. And I pictured what
we'd look like if you could see us from above: two sisters,
sleeping across from each other, same position, just flipped.
Back to back.

Tempest and I were mirror twins; our cells had decided
at the last possible moment to divide into two people in the
womb. So that meant we shared everything, but flipped. The
part in my hair was on the right; hers was on the left. I was
right-handed; she was a lefty. That kind of thing.

Opposites.

She'd been smaller than me at birth. She had trouble
breathing, with a hole in her heart that meant surgery when
we were not even a year old. She had a scar on her chest that
I didn't have. It was pink and raised, a bit shiny, but faded so
many years later. She breathed just fine now.

I was the one who developed asthma as we grew up.

Opposites, but more than that: Connected. Intertwined.
The same.

But things had changed this year somehow; a weird fric-
tion had crept in between us. And I didn't like it.

I heaved a sigh and heard the sound of Bones's paws thumping on the bedroom's wooden floor. He jumped up and found his spot on the foot of my bed, but not before he pressed his wet nose into my face and held it there. "Good night, boy," I told him, scratching the scruff of his neck, sleep nudging in around my thoughts.

I dreamt of the pleasant snapping sound the peachy-orange canvas of Pa Charlie's carnival tents made in the wind, and the sweet smell of Molly-Mae's Georgia-famous kettle corn, and of course, the droning, whirring, buzzing bells and horns of the carnival rides.

And then I saw something that looked like a bracelet or a watch made out of paper, the stiff kind like index cards. It didn't quite make sense. It was yellow and ragged, flipping over in the breeze, dancing and turning across a field of milk-weed. I watched it for a good long time, until it fluttered high on a gust of wind, and it floated up into the sky, toward darkening purple clouds and a too-large blood-orange moon.

3

Even Bones was still asleep when I woke the next morning. Glory, hallelujah, how did a dog snore so loud? Like a warthog working a buzz saw.

I looked over at my still-sleeping sister. She had kicked all the blankets off her bed, like she always did.

When I flipped over to go back to sleep, Bones woke up and then whimpered all pathetic-like right in my ear.

"Okay, okay," I grumbled. I got up, slipping my feet into my flip-flops.

I threw on a semi-clean flannel shirt and took Bones out into the backyard. The dew was cold on my feet, and a little sliver of moon—a hangnail moon, as Pa Charlie always called it—was high in the lavender sky.

Bones went on his morning walkabout: through the vegetable garden and around Mama's rusty weather vane collection. He sniffed near the chicken coop, our old cat's favorite place to lie in the sun. I wondered if Bones missed that cranky cat, how she used to bite at his ears if he was in a spot she considered hers.

Bones spent a little time circling the big oak, giving his collar a couple of extra scratches, as well as his left ear. Then he did his business behind Dad's toolshed, his nose in the air like he couldn't believe he had to work for his privacy.

I shivered in the weird morning coolness. My ears perked when I heard Mama's voice from the kitchen, and something about the tone froze me in place.

I couldn't make out her words. But I did catch Daddy's reply: "Tomorrow?"

"He's making a circus jump soon from Dunwoody." I heard Mama's voice now as she moved closer to the back door.

Dad sighed. "Okay, Genevieve. If you think that's best."

"If we're really going to allow this, then we need to get it over with. Before I rethink it."

"We don't have to," Daddy answered. His voice had that wrung-out sound to it. "But we can hope that nothing will come of it. Do the girls ever ask you about Grania, anyway?"

"No," Mama answered.

Aunt Grania? What did Mama's world-traveling, never-around sister have to do with anything? I tiptoed to the back steps, straining my ears.

I caught only a snatch of what Daddy said next. "—more than they're letting on?"

Mama answered, "I think Tempest might."

What?

Mama continued then, her voice so small I really had to concentrate to hear it, and I only caught snippets. She must've moved farther away from the door, toward the pantry. "It—terrible—never my choice."

My ears were pricked and I was standing stock-still right outside the door now. But that was all I got. Bits and pieces of something. What was terrible? What wasn't her choice? And what in the jelly sandwich did Tempest maybe know that I didn't?

"By the way," Daddy said, passing close to the back door, his voice easy to hear now. "Are the girls supposed to know yet about Molly-Mae and your dad?"

Mama mumbled a response, and I strained my ears, but after that the only sounds were the breakfast ones: the hiss of the coffeemaker, the pad of Daddy's old slippers on the wood floor, the clink of a sugar spoon.

I made a big fuss coming back in the house with Bones, trying to show that I was having a totally normal morning and hadn't been listening to their totally abnormal conversation. I knew better than to put Mama and Daddy in the hot seat and straight-out ask them what kind of secrets they were keeping from us. All it would earn me was a lecture on eavesdropping.

So instead, I said, "Piggly Wiggly has Bones's flea medicine on BOGO. Saw it in the paper."

Mama and Daddy had a quick conversation just with their eyes, probably wondering how much I'd heard.

"No way me and Tempest can take Bones with us to Peachtree?" I asked, knowing what the answer would be. I bent down and scratched at his scraggly ears.

"Tempest and I," Mama corrected. "And, no, I don't think so, Tally."

"Well, he's got a flea or two," I told her.

"I'll take care of him," Mama said. Then she put her coffee on the counter. "By the way, honey, Dr. Fran called last night."

"Yeah?" I edged toward the stairs, wanting to go mull over what I had overheard.

"She asked if I'd tell you that you were right about Winnie."

"Oh, okay."

"What did you know about Winnie?" Mama asked. "That's the new greyhound she's sheltering, right?"

"Yeah. I just thought . . . I could tell she was favoring her left back paw. Asked Dr. Fran to take a look at it."

"That's my girl," Mama said.

And I took off up the stairs, Bones at my heels.

When I got back to our room, Tempest was still asleep. She looked so cold, knees drawn up to her chest, that I instinctively went to pull the covers back over her.

I concentrated again.

Wake up.

Do as I say.

Nothing. Not even a hitch in her breath or a wrinkle of her nose. I grabbed the blankets at the bottom of her bed and began to pull them up over her, but something stopped me.

There it was again.

That weird thrum of pressure—like yesterday in the science lab, but not as strong. Just a whisper of it, making my back teeth feel like I'd chewed tinfoil.

The air around me vibrated like a bell just rung. I leaned closer to Tempest, and it got a little worse.

For a second, just a flash, I couldn't see Tempest clearly. The air between us shimmered. My vision bent in waves, like heat coming off the Georgia asphalt in July. I blinked and it went away. But there was still that little hum, a pressure in my ears.

I dropped the blanket onto my sister and took a step back.

It lessened.

I took another step back, and it darn near disappeared. What in the green beans was going on?

I looked around our room. Did Tempest have some kind of weird equipment set up? Had she accidentally left something on?

Could it be one of Tempest's gadgets gone awry? I bent and sifted through her box of junk at the foot of the bed, lifting a few of her doodads this way and that, eyeing each of her gadgets— but, no, nothing seemed to be producing that strange hum.

I only felt it when I went near my sister.

Then I had a strange thought: maybe it was one of her gadgets gone *right*.

Was Tempest doing this on purpose? Had she created some invention designed to push me away? Some kind of revenge over our fight about Mary Anning, or some other imagined slight?

The idea made my knees wobbly. "Whoa," I whispered into the quiet space of our room.

Tempest didn't stir.

I looked at my sister, at her calm face, her hair spread out on the pillow.

Could she really be pushing me away somehow, on purpose? Counteracting our natural pull?

Did she have anything in her hands? Some kind of remote control that might trigger the force? Like some invisible dog collar for a wayward twin sister, buzzing me if I got too close?

No. There was nothing. Not that I could see. I hunched over her, peering at her face, and suddenly, now, there was no weird feeling left.

Just Tempest and me. As always.

I could almost tell myself I'd imagined this whole weirdo thing.

I reached out to shake her gently on the shoulder, but before I even touched her, she said, "I'm up. Quit staring at me."

"I . . . um—"

"What is it?" She opened her eyes and sat up.

I don't know why, but I didn't say what I'd been thinking. I told myself it was all a fluke. Instead, I just said, "We're meeting Pa Charlie tomorrow."

"What? Already?"

"Yeah."

"That's soon." She stretched.

I took a deep breath, then went and dragged our big suit-case out of the closet. "Once we get finished packing, we'll go say goodbye to Marisol. Maybe Dr. Fran too."

"Okay," Tempest said, getting up from bed. She pulled her tattered shoebox from under her bed and placed it on our desk. It made a bunch of clinking and clanking noises as she began adding some of the other equipment from our bookshelf.

"By the way, Tempest, did you know there's something going on between Pa Charlie and Molly-Mae?"

"Sure. They're sweet on each other, Tally."

"What? What else do you know that I don't?"

"Lots of things, I bet. But what do you mean specifically?"

"About why Mama and Daddy aren't coming with us to the carnival? About why they're acting weird." I narrowed my eyes into slits.

"I think I dreamt about Aunt Grania last night. She wore lots of jangly bracelets."

"We've never even met her," I said. "What does Grania Greenly have to do with anything?"

Tempest shrugged. "I don't know." And I figured she was telling the truth. She always pulled on her eyelashes in this weird way when she was trying to get away with a fib.

"What are you working on now?" I asked her.

"Not exactly sure yet," she answered. "Has something to do with the tides." She picked up a small gear and held it to the light, then dropped it back into her box and picked up what looked like a watch face.

I was about to tell Tempest more of what I'd heard our parents discussing, but then she picked up some kind of a circular metal thing with sawtooth edges. She turned it around in her hand, looking at it so very closely I thought she was going to go cross-eyed, and . . . I don't know. What exactly had I heard?

Just enough to worry my stomach into a knot.

Anyway, I got back to packing.

4

"Pa Charlie!" we both called out the car window. As soon as the car rumbled to a stop on the Dunwoody carnival grounds, Tempest and I jumped out. He waved from across the lot, near the ancient carousel. My heart pinged against my ribs. I loved our Pa Charlie. He always seemed to look upon me with kinder eyes than the rest of the world.

It was late evening and the crescent moon shone high in the sky, but the crew wasn't tearing the carnival down yet. The place was in full swing: game bells ringing, lights flashing, rides whirring. Customers laughed and hooted and hollered, forgetting that they were blowing their hard-earned money on fool's games. Clusters of little kids ran around with Kool-Aid mustaches, trailing their licorice ropes behind them. A knot of teenagers huddled around the most popular ride, the Spaceship 3000. It spun so fast that Fat Sam, who wasn't fat at all even though we called him that, had to keep his supply of barf dust right under the ride's milk-crate ticket stand.

A waft of spun sugar blew past us, some kids were complaining at the dart-throwing booth, and Arnold Shutes, who we called Arnie the Carnie, gave us a wink as we walked onto the midway. Tempest and I waved to Hames, who stood behind the ping-pong-ball goldfish booth, a cigar dangling from his lips. "Hey, y'all!" he called as he counted out quarters from the change apron around his waist. A newbie running the potato-sack slide looked up from his post, and a couple of carnies waved from near the Ferris wheel, one of them leaning on the old iron lever. I waved back, but I couldn't remember their names from last year.

And then I saw Molly-Mae over by the Candy Wagon, her hair a white beehive that mirrored the shape and wispiness of cotton candy. "Girls! How you been?" she yelled.

"Hey, Miss Molly!" I called, but now Pa Charlie was grabbing Tempest and me into a bear hug.

"My girls!" he said in his honey-smooth voice, and he pulled away to give us a good sizing up. "My golden girls," he said. "You're taller." He gave us his best scrutinizing look, his bushy, gray eyebrows meeting in the middle. "And you're string beans. We need to feed y'all. Molly-Mae, could you make us up a junk buffet for Tempest and Tally here?" Pa called.

"Hi, Dad," Mama said as she caught up and gave him a kiss on his bearded jowl.

"Charlie!" Dad said, shaking Pa's hand.

"We missed you," I told Pa Charlie, wrapping my arms around him for another squeeze. Lawdy, he had an enormous middle, and I loved smelling that Pa Charlie smell: pipe tobacco, the outdoors, and good old sweat.

"Your sister here's been writing me letters all spring. What's the matter with your writing hand?" he asked me, holding my right hand up in the air and pressing it up to his gigantic palm.

"Nothing," I said, but I shot Tempest a look before changing the subject. "How's Antique?"

Pa Charlie motioned toward the peach and green canvases of the petting zoo tent, and I pulled on Tempest. "Let's go see him."

We left Mama and Daddy hugging and catching up on gossip with Pa and hustled toward our pony.

"Really, Tally," Tempest said. "You don't have to be so abrupt all the time."

"What are you talking about?" I said, shoving the canvas aside, loving how familiar the rough fabric felt in my fingers.

"Pa wanted to talk to us."

"He did?"

"Tally, maybe you should give people half as much attention as you give your animals. How about that?"

"Tempest, replace animals with gears and batteries, and I could say the same to you."

"Hey."

"Hey nothing," I wanted to say. But I let it go, because I had that familiar thrill inside my belly, growing and shooting out through the rest of my body. Every summer at the carnival was an adventure waiting to happen. And now, here we were. With my animals. The alpacas from Morrow's Farm that came on the road for the summer. The strange little wolf pups Daddy had told us about that Pa had nursed back to health after he found them motherless and starving in the farmland behind his creek a few weeks ago. The two grumpy turkeys named Salt and Pepper.

And, in the far stall, there he was: Antique. The pride of Peachtree. At least to me.

A few summers back, Pa and Daddy had gone to an auction, hoping to add to the petting zoo, and they came back with a beautiful, midnight-black gelding.

He took to me right away. Tempest had been too busy with her telescope that summer, and sure, I fed him sugar cubes from the get-go, but that doesn't totally explain exactly how much we liked each other from day one. Pa Charlie likes to say that animals don't get bothered as much as people do by prickliness. He said that over and over to Mama and Daddy that summer, having a good laugh, and I knew they were talking about me. But I didn't care, because here was this beautiful animal, and Pa Charlie acted like he was mine.

When Pa Charlie told me that I got to name him, I nearly burst with pride. Tempest hadn't seemed too bothered— though, truthfully, I kind of wanted her to be.

I tried to think of the best, catchiest name around. Antique Jones.

Sometimes we have to live with our mistakes.

"Antique," I said, clicking my tongue and brushing my hand against the slats of his stall.

His ears pricked up and he raised his head from his feed bucket. His nostrils flared a few times, and then he turned his head so his left eye met mine. He sashayed toward me, pressing his face against the bars, and I stroked his velvety nose. I could feel exactly how much he had missed me.

"Well, there ya go," Tempest said, giving him a friendly pat too. I had kind of forgotten she was there.

"How you doing, Antique?" I asked, and he whinnied in recognition. I palmed him a peppermint from my pocket, and he took off, prancing around his stall like it was Christmas morning.

I let myself in with him, grabbing one of the brushes hanging just outside the stall. "You been missing me?" I asked him, as I worked the brush slowly through his mane. Antique bobbed his head in a fashion that I took to mean yes.

"Well, I have plans for us, Antique. We'll take a ride down to the shore, once we go south. We're gonna have ourselves a summer." I marveled at the different shades of black in Antique's coat: shiny coal-black, dark and dusty near-gray, the smooth silver-color of his eyes. He was every bit as beautiful as I'd remembered.

I was deep into telling Antique about my school year when I heard a sound behind me. "Tempest?" I called, but she didn't answer, and I didn't know if she had left while I was talking with Antique, or if she was playing a prank on me.

"Boo!"

To his credit, Antique barely flinched. I, however, fell back on my butt, square into Antique's hay, letting out a howl. This tall, skinny stranger had scared me but good. I was just about to lay into whoever this was when I got a good look at the smile taunting me, and I stopped, flummoxed.

This stinkweed of a man looked like Digger Swanson. He had that same messy, just-this-side-of-blond hair, that off-center dimple in his chin. That goofy grin, the gap between his teeth wide enough to fit a popsicle stick between. I got up and brushed off my butt, squinting at him.

"Holy kudzu, Digger?" I said. "You've grown about three feet!"

"Yes ma'am, eating my vegetables. And good to see you too, Tally Jo." He punched me lightly on the shoulder. I rubbed at the spot, glaring at him. I didn't know why, but I didn't like that he had caught me off guard, that he looked different, that he had gone and grown partially up without me around to ignore it. I didn't like the notion that I had something or someone to catch up to.

"Have you seen Tempest?" I asked.

"Yeah, she's out eating all the junk Molly-Mae cooked up for y'all."

I turned to finish brushing Antique, irked.

"Saw your daddy over by the rides," I said to Digger.

"Yep, Fat Sam'll be here forever. So will I."

"Humph."

"What's got your knickers twisted, Tally? Thought you'd be happy to get back."

"I am happy," I told him. "You don't need to be sneaking up on a girl, is all."

"Whatever you say." Digger put his hands up in surrender. Then he said, slowly, "You know, my mother's not here though. They got a divorce this past winter."

"I heard," I said.

"My mom's already got herself a new boyfriend. But, you never know, my parents might get back together. Stranger things have happened."

"True." I wasn't sure what else I should say.

"You and Tempest want to sneak out tonight and go fishing in Cranberry Lake?"

"Nah," I told him. "Our mama and daddy are staying tonight, but they're leaving in the morning. We better hang around."

"Oh." Digger kicked at the dirt floor. "Maybe in a couple days then, when we're in St. Simons. We can fish the Intracoastal. Or go to one of the black-sand beaches."

I felt lighter then, and I gave Digger a good, proper smile. "I love St. Simons Island."

"We'll have to go out to the beach. Maybe we'll find another stingray washed up."

"Maybe you'll pee your pants again," I told him, smiling. He laughed, a deep, one-note guffaw. There was that same Digger magic in it, from every other summer of my life. And just like that, I forgot about how he looked all different.

"Maybe you'll finally admit you threw that water balloon."

"Never." I wrapped my arms around Antique's neck, and I laughed good and hard, happy to be back.

And we were just Digger and Tally again.

5

Pa Charlie did something he never does: he postponed the teardown and moving of the carnival so that we all could have the night with Mama and Daddy before they left.

As the Peachtree Carnival family sat around the campfire, surrounded by the half dozen rusted-out, paint-peeling trailers that housed the lot of us every summer, I felt warm and cozy. I nestled into my lawn chair next to Digger's, one of Pa Charlie's old quilts tucked around my shoulders. Granny Greenly had sewn it many years ago, before she passed. A blue-and-green geometric print, it was the perfect size to cuddle under, just the right weight and thickness for a cool Georgia summer evening.

My belly was full of elephant ears and hot dogs, and my eyelids grew heavy as I watched the folks around me drinking their root beer floats, trading stories and jokes. Pa's big belly jiggled when he laughed, and Tempest scooted her chair closer to him when he lit his pipe. I knew why; I liked the smell of it too, even if it did irritate my asthma.

"Do the girls know the big news?" Pa Charlie asked, talking around the pipe in his mouth.

"No, they don't," Mama answered with a tight smile.

Pa Charlie chuckled and announced, "Well, the glorious news is that Grania is joining the carnival this summer."

I sat up straight, and I saw shock register on Tempest's face too. "Tally, did you know?" she asked.

"No, I didn't." *But I heard Mama talking about something, earlier. Something strange.* I shot Mama a look.

She was smiling. She was, but it wasn't an authentic Mama smile. It had a Sad Mama quality to it, like she was trying too hard.

And something suddenly occurred to me. Tempest and I knew of Aunt Grania, of course. She wasn't a secret, exactly. More like a legend, or a mythical creature, someone who only seemed real by way of her spotty phone calls and the unannounced packages that showed up at random times, holding nesting dolls from Russia, jade chess pieces from Shanghai, or whatever else. The fact we'd never met her . . . well, it had never demanded a lot of attention, so we didn't give it much.

But I knew Mama and Aunt Grania were mirror twins, just like Tempest and me. Had they been close at one time?

Never my choice.

Isn't that what I'd heard Mama say to Daddy? Did it have something to do with Aunt Grania?

"When is she coming?" Tempest asked. "And why this summer?"

"We don't know for sure. Grania's never absolute about these things. She'll probably just show up," Pa said.

Fat Sam said to Mama, "I still remember your old act with your sister. It was really something."

"What act?" Tempest asked.

Mama answered, "Nothing, really. Just a hobby. Grania and I used to cut out these garlands and hand them out to kids. It was just—"

"So, are you going to stay to see her?" I interrupted.

Mama's smile faltered. "I don't think so, Tally."

"Why in the world not? Don't you want to be here when we finally get to meet your own twin?"

I watched as Mama took a deep breath, closing her eyes against something. And then when she opened them, her Sad Mama look took over completely. "It's a complicated situation, Tally Jo." Daddy grabbed Mama's hand.

"Why can't you just explain it?" Tempest asked. She blinked once, twice, three slow times.

"When you're older."

"Why are you acting so mysterious?" I asked Mama, and Daddy gave a hard shake of his head.

Nobody answered me.

Pa Charlie got up to feed another log to the fire, the rest of us sitting thick in an awkward silence. I thought about Mama saying Tempest and I were growing up. Is this what getting older was gonna be like? Ignoring the tough questions? Never having to explain a lickety-split thing?

Pa Charlie reclaimed his seat and said, "Play us a tune," to Fat Sam. In a matter of moments, Fat Sam had his banjo out and Molly-Mae was singing along with him, her voice teetering and tottering over the notes of a familiar country song.

Digger leaned over toward me, his voice low. "You never met your aunt?"

"No."

"How come?"

I shrugged. "My grandparents got divorced when Mama and Aunt Grania were in high school—Aunt Grania went and lived with Pa Charlie, and Mama stayed with my Granny Greenly. After high school, our mama went to New York on an art scholarship. Aunt Grania travels a lot—she writes for magazines." Digger gave me a look. "So we've never met her, not in person."

"Sounds kinda weird."

I shrugged.

"You don't think it's weird that they split up?" Digger asked.

"My grandparents? No. Lots of people get divorced."

"No, I mean your aunt and your mom. They're twins, like you and Tempest, right? And they split up, and never see each other?"

I nodded and shrugged again. Yes, I did think it was weird . . . *now*. Why I'd never thought about it until this night was a good question.

Suddenly, I was too tired to worry about any of it. I nestled deep down in my lawn chair and curled into Pa's old quilt.

I watched the fire as it burned and crackled, smoked and surged. Arnie had his harmonica out and he played along with Fat Sam's banjo. The latest tune was slow and tender, plucking at my heart, making me look at that lonely place inside me.

I was hit deep in my ribs then with an image from last summer: Tempest and I sitting close, sharing one lawn chair. She had her head thrown back in laughter as I relayed my latest prank on Digger.

Fat Sam's banjo was lulling me into a melancholy mood, the slow melody sharpening my sadness to a point. I watched Tempest across the fire pit. She and Molly-Mae were talking. Tempest blinked too slowly, a time or two. She pressed the back of her knuckles to her lips—another tell. What had her worried?

But my eyelids were growing heavy in the mesmerizing crackle and spark of the campfire, so I let them close.

"Psst." Mama pulled gently on my ponytail. "Daddy and I are taking off, Tally Jo. Just wanted to say goodbye."

I stood up from my lawn chair, pulling the quilt over my shoulders, and exchanged hugs with my parents. Mama and Daddy were leaving us here by ourselves—leaving us without telling us exactly why. It was strange, in that queasy-feeling way that reminded me that things weren't done changing yet.

And if this past year with Tempest was any indication, change wasn't exactly fabulous.

I realized in that moment that I might get lonely here at the carnival, without Mama and Daddy. I would be with my sister, sure, but I might still be lonely. What a terrible, awful thought.

"You be good, Tally," Daddy said.

"I will," I said, rubbing at my eyes. The fire had died down to a few glowing embers. Only a handful of people still sat around the circle: Pa Charlie and Hames, deep in discussion, and Molly-Mae singing in her trilling bird voice along to Fat Sam's still-strumming banjo.

"Watch out for your sister," Daddy said.

"I always do."

Mama pursed her lips. "Remember your manners around here. Listen to your pa. And call me if you . . . you know, if you need anything. If you aren't feeling right or if anything comes up."

Mama's eyes skittered away from mine, making me feel something was askew. "What do you mean?"

"Just if your asthma acts up or anything," Daddy answered, too fast.

"Now, where'd your sister go off to?" Mama asked. I shrugged but Mama and Daddy were meandering over toward the rest of the camp to say their goodbyes.

Digger appeared at my shoulder. "Come with me," he said, all quiet, looking around like he was trying to get away with something. "Just act like we're going to the animal tent." He yanked on my hand and pulled me in that direction. I dropped my quilt into my chair and took off after Digger.

Once we were out of sight, he veered off and led me across a rugged field of elephant grass behind the midway. I nearly tripped and killed myself over some kind of old motor that had been left out there to rust, but I kept trudging after Digger, trying to puzzle out how somebody's bones and skin could stretch out and accommodate all that new height in such a short amount of time.

"Hold up, Digger!" I yelled at him.

"Come on, Tally."

He rounded a big dirt hill littered with cinder blocks and construction dregs. "Look at what I got here," he crooned then, pulling a plastic grocery bag of junk out from the front pocket of his hoodie.

"What is it?"

Digger waggled his eyebrows at me.

"Holy roses," I said as he opened the bag and showed me a whole mess of fireworks. "How'd you get these past Pa Charlie? He hates firecrackers."

"I got my ways." He shoved the bag back into his hoodie pocket. "Come on. Let's get farther away. We'll shoot some off."

"Yeah." I followed through the field, across a muddy little creek, the crickets chirping loudly, the wind telling me the story of the coming summer as it danced across my chilled cheeks. The crescent moon perched in the sky, illuminating the night just enough, giving a little hopeful edge to the darkness.

Digger finally stopped near a stand of old oaks, kudzu and Spanish moss hanging between them like ancient hammocks. "This'll do," he said, all matter-of-factly.

I chuckled and snatched the matches from his hands. "Me first. Give me one of the big ones."

He handed me a cherry bomb, and I struck the match, relishing the quick sulfur scent. I lit the fuse, and I chucked the firework out into the open. It exploded, the bang loud and satisfying. He quickly moved across the field and began to level a launching pad in the dirt for some of the brocades—the kind that shoot up and burst open in a big circular *pow* of color. Tempest liked to call them chrysanthemums.

I placed one of these into the dirt Digger had loosened up. He lit the wick and then we ran back to the stand of trees to watch the firework explode. This one lit up in the sky, round and bright, a green and yellow canopy of candle flames, rendering Digger and me speechless. The colors were so . . . alive. I hurried to set up another in the dirt, while Digger tossed another cherry bomb behind me. I flinched when it blew, even though I knew it was coming.

"You getting soft, Tally Jo?" he called.

"Not on your life, Digger."

"Here," he said, crouching down next to me. "Let's do a bunch of 'em." So we lined up five of the brocades in a row and lit the fuses quickly, one after another. Then we hightailed it.

The light show was really something. Purples and reds, blues and whites, and a couple of umbrella-shaped oranges and yellows. The sparks erupted in the sky, dazzling. They dangled there for a moment before tapering off into nothingness.

I found myself wishing Tempest was with us. *She would love this*, I thought.

Or would she? She would've last summer. But now, she spent more and more time on her own, with her box of bolts and her trips to the junkyard for parts.

I shook the thought away, the smile fading from my face, and I knew Digger's eyes were on me.

"You're different," he said. He lit a bottle rocket and tossed it away from us.

"No I'm not," I said, scowling. "You're different."

"I guess I am," he said, and I could hear something in his voice, something new. I didn't like it. "Playing on the eighth-grade baseball team next fall," he boasted. "My curveball is the best in three counties." He sort of stuck his chest out when he said this.

"You're still a pain in the butt to me."

And with that, he laughed, his car-engine laugh, and he sounded like my Digger again.

That's when Tempest appeared out of nowhere, scaring me half to death. "Why'd you leave me behind?" she said, folding her arms over her chest.

I shrugged.

"We didn't know where you were," Digger said.

"Fat Sam let me look through his old bicycle parts."

"Find anything good?" I asked. I was trying to be interested in Tempest's quest for gadgets galore.

Tempest nodded. "A vintage speedometer. Some cogs and ball bearings." She shrugged and started to root around in the bag of fireworks. Digger took off across the field to set up a line of bottle rockets.

"Here, let me light that for you," I said, striking a match for Tempest, who had chosen a big chrysanthemum.

But when I got close to her, there it was. That strange something again, just like that day in the science lab.

But stronger. It exploded between us, pushed me back from her in a jolt of energy, a hissing *whoosh* of air. I nearly fell back on my behind. I scuttled backward three steps, four, and the force still brushed my hair back. The match went out, and I stopped dead still.

"What in the world is this?" I asked. "You got some invention brushing me back, Tally? You pulling some kind of prank?"

"No . . ."

Digger's bottle-rocket succession exploded and the noise jolted me.

Tempest and I stood about two feet away from each other, and I took another step closer. It wasn't like I *couldn't* do it; I could. But it was hard, like trying to propel myself through a wind tunnel. The air between Tempest and me, it was thick and fairly pulsing.

I ripped out another match and worked to strike it on the matchbook cover while Tempest eyed me all suspicious-like. I couldn't get the darn match to strike.

"Let me try," Tempest said, and then she reached out for the book in my hand. And I could see her struggle, see her eyes widen at how hard it was to push through the space toward me.

"What the heck is—"

But I didn't finish my sentence, because as she reached toward me, and even before her hand grasped the matchbook, I watched one of the matches spark a weird, blue-purple color. In a blink, the whole book caught fire, every single match in one big hot flame.

"Whoa," Digger yelped from where he stood nearby.

I hurled the fiery matchbook away, and it landed in a patch of brush near Tempest. The dried grass and brush crackled and caught fire. Tempest took several steps away from me, eyeing me closely.

"You better cut this out," I said. "You're—"

"It's not me." She busied herself stomping out the fire, and Digger joined in, muttering to himself.

I stared at them, scared to get too close.

When the flames were out, Digger turned his attention back to me. "What was that? You forget how to light a match?"

"I . . . um . . ." I let my voice trail off as I backed even farther away from Tempest, needing to lessen the pressure on my lungs. I snatched my inhaler from my pocket, took two long pulls. It was still there, coming at me in waves, settling between my eyes like a bad case of brain freeze. I didn't know what to do. I couldn't get a breath. "You got a drink of water?" I squeaked.

"Yeah," Digger said, digging into his bag.

Tempest looked at me all funny. "I just remembered, I gotta go back . . ." she stammered. "I promised Pa Charlie . . ." She turned back for camp, and my breathing came easier with each bit of distance Tempest put between us.

Digger's eyes were full of questions. "Here." He gave me a bottle of water, and I took a pull. I felt better already though.

Digger watched me, but I just ignored him like it was my job, draining the bottle of water.

Instead of peppering me with the twenty questions I was sure he wanted to ask, Digger let it drop.

Wonders never cease.

He took off toward the Spanish oak near the base of the hill. I watched Digger's silhouette as he climbed up into its massive, kudzu-covered branches.

"Come on, Tally, you're missing the view!" he yelled.

"Uh-huh," I called. I ran toward the tree, but when I got up into the branches of that old oak, it wasn't the view that drew my attention. Not the bright sickle moon in the sky or the lit-up constellations in the wide-open country sky. No, it was the tiny, disappearing figure of my sister running back to camp, small and alone, a silhouette against the lights of the carnival and flame of the campfire, her pigtails bouncing with each step she took.

6

Tempest pretended to be sleeping when I got back to our trailer—or our pod, as we called it, on account of it was this pod-shaped add-on that Pa Charlie always pulled behind his monster of a motor home. You couldn't quite stand up in it, but it was ours. A twin bed on each side, some built-in drawers at the foot of each. There was a small, square window in the back, between our beds, and a ladybug suncatcher—one of two we'd made the summer before—still hung there. I squinted, trying to tell if that one had been mine or Tempest's. I couldn't tell.

I stripped out of my clothes and pulled on some pajamas, trying to feel out the atmosphere in our pod, bracing myself for . . . whatever. But there was nothing weird going on. Whatever had been between us seemed to have evaporated somehow.

When I finally pulled up the sheet, right to my nose—and it smelled like I remembered: campfire and Tide—I realized I wasn't tired, but keyed up from all that had happened. "Why are you pretending to be sleeping?" I said into the dark.

Tempest rolled over, but she said nothing. I sighed.

"Are you worrying about what happened with the matches?" I waited. And just when I thought she wasn't going to answer, she did.

"Are you?"

"Well, this all began when you started working with the magnets at school. Maybe this is a result of one of your gadgets or—"

"No."

"Maybe you don't even realize you're doing it. It's like a side effect of—"

"No, it's not."

I didn't know what to say. I wanted to say something horrible, like *Maybe you're doing this in some twin-magic way. Like your mind trick when you kept me from punching Bradley. Maybe you're pushing me away on purpose. Because you're tired of me. Because you're too busy with your new inventions, your new hobbies, your new life. The one that doesn't have time for me.*

I didn't say it though.

Tempest turned over again, and I could see that she was facing me now, even though it was dark. I couldn't quite make out her features, but her eyes reflected a sliver of the moonlight coming in our little pod window. Tempest's voice dropped to a whisper. "Remember our dog-walking business?"

"How could I forget?"

"You mean the rhubarb incident? Come on, that was fun."

"Fun? You could say that." I chuckled, thinking of Mr. Ku's rottweiler and its penchant for chewing on the rhubarb growing behind Mrs. Culpepper's garage. "How were we supposed to know that the leaves of rhubarb were poison?"

"I never saw purple barf before."

"We had, what, seventeen dogs at once?"

"Eighteen if you count that mangy Chihuahua."

"Seventeen and a half, maybe."

Tempest giggled.

"We were a well-oiled machine back then, weren't we, Tempest?" Those had been the days, both of us working on something together, all day, every day, all summer long, inseparable.

Tempest spoke even more softly now. "Tally, you know I only did stuff like that . . . Well, I did it 'cause it was fun to do *with you.*"

I sat up straight then, leaning toward my sister. "And it was fun to do stuff together, wasn't it?" I wanted her to say it, to admit she missed us. To agree that we could find a way to get ourselves back to how we were.

"Tally. Those things though . . . they never really wound my clock. They weren't *my* interests."

"Oh," I said, leaning back on my pillow.

"I was just always being . . . your assistant. But eventually I had to get brave enough to become me. Not just a version of you. You understand what I'm getting at?"

"Not really."

"You don't want to understand."

We lay in silence then, for what seemed like a long time, listening to the cricket song outside. Me, trying to control my temper, Tempest being quiet. Oh, how I missed Bones.

I found myself thinking about Mama and Aunt Grania, about what I'd overheard Mama saying. I felt like I was truly understanding the root of her Sad Mama moments.

"Never my choice," she'd said.

Had Mama been talking about her separation from her sister? Had Aunt Grania slowly grown away from Mama, then up and took off, leaving her for good? Traveling the world, writing her zany magazine articles about crystals and acupuncture and who knows what else? Did Aunt Grania flee into her own grown-up life, never looking back? Just completely forgetting how to make room for her sister in her exciting adventures?

Or had they argued about something? Right then, lying in the pod, I tried to imagine what in the jelly sandwich could've been bad enough for Mama and Aunt Grania to fight about that they wouldn't want to see each other anymore. I tried out a few theories: Had they fought about who would go with who after their parents' divorce? Had they fought over money for their colleges, or maybe over a super-handsome, motorcycle-riding boyfriend who ran a mobile kitten shelter?

It was hard to imagine, really it was. But not impossible.

A year ago, I wouldn't have been able to imagine anything like that at all.

This year, I almost . . . *almost* . . . could.

Tempest turned back over and brought her knees up, curling herself into her sleeping position.

We shared a lot of things, being identical: looks, genetics, clothes, friends, living quarters, underwear, even. But as I lay there in my bed, that first night back at Pa Charlie's, I found myself thinking more and more about the day before kindergarten when Mama told us she was putting us in separate classes. "So you can have your own life too," she'd told us then, her smile faltering just a little.

"But we're the same," was all I could come up with. Tempest had been silent.

"Come here," Mama had said, and she'd pulled out a bottle of nail polish. "Give me your index fingers. Both of y'all."

We obliged, and I remembered being so surprised when Mama brushed the paint onto the pads of our pointer fingers, instead of on the nails. Then she'd pressed our fingerprints onto an index card, side by side. "Look closely."

I'd studied them, narrowing my eyes. "They're different!" I had said, so surprised after six years of sharing everything with my sister. Our secret sign language of our toddler years, the same bed half the time, the freckle under our eye—hers on the left, mine on the right.

"They're kind of the same," Tempest had said. And I'd snatched the index card again and brought it close to my face to study. The prints swirled up from the bottom in the same fashion, and then whirled counterclockwise. But Tempest's print was more scrunched, with a few more vertical lines off to the left side. I studied that card closely. Had Tempest smudged hers when she pressed her thumb onto the paper, or something? I mean, shouldn't we have the same fingerprints?

I didn't know much about stuff then, but I did know that Tempest having a different fingerprint than me seemed weird and wrong, in a way that my six-year-old brain couldn't really put into words.

"Mama, no," I said, shoving the index card back at her.

"Yes," she explained. "You are not *exactly* the same. You have your own personalities. You are your own person."

I'd scrunched my face into my best angry scowl and aimed a kick right at Mama's shin.

I'd been grounded from the television for an entire week because of that.

Then Tempest had bawled like a baby on the first day of school, and Mrs. Hunter had to pry us apart. I, on the other hand, had just narrowed my eyes at Mama and comforted Tempest, trying so hard to be strong.

That first night back in our pod, I fell asleep wondering about that conversation. Wondering about Tempest and me. About Aunt Grania and Mama.

About the matches. About the growing space between us.

7

I halfway woke to the breakdown clatter of the carnival rides, tents, and attractions right outside our pod. I fought waking up, pulling the blankets over my head.

But, of course, I couldn't get back to sleep. I made myself get out of bed, grumbling under my breath the whole while. I stood and stretched, and my eye caught the red picture frame on the wall of our pod, opposite the lone window.

That red frame had been there forever, nailed to the wall and secured with heaps of blue sticky tack so it would stay where it was supposed to despite the bumps and thumps of traveling. Inside the picture frame was a silhouette garland my mother had made when she was a kid.

It was just a fancy version of a paper-doll chain, like the ones we all learned to make in school by folding up a piece of paper just exactly right, and cutting out a stick figure. Then, when you unfolded the paper, accordion style, there were a dozen stick figures, all identical, all holding hands.

It was like that, but fancier, more beautiful, and incredibly intricate. It was nothing like the plain old paper dolls I could do. Anyone could tell, with just one glance, that Mama was an artist.

The garland showed a pair of girls. They were bent toward each other at the waist, their noses nearly touching, one heel kicked out behind each of them, forever frozen in the midst of sharing a secret. Their hands held on to an umbrella between them, their pigtails caught mid-swing, defying gravity. The swoop of the girls' eyelashes was a thing of beauty: so smooth, so tiny, so impossibly fine.

The pair of them repeated six times inside that red frame.

But I always liked to think that it really continued outside of that frame. Pair after pair, on and on. Forever.

At first glance, you would think the girls were identical, but if you looked closely, you'd see there were differences. One of the girls leans in a bit more than the other. Her hand sits higher on the umbrella than the other's. She's sheltering her sister from the rain.

I stepped closer to the frame, thinking of what Fat Sam had said last night around the fire, about Mama and Aunt Grania having an act, cutting out garlands. Suddenly, I was curious.

Had they *both* made these silhouettes?

I studied it closely. I searched the paper, looking for a signature, but found none. However, when I squinted, I could barely see the shadow of writing through the paper, as if something was written on the back.

I dug my fingers behind that red frame and I pulled it off the wall.

I flipped the frame over. There was Mama's handwriting, all loops and even lettering—elegant, just like her. It was clear the entire back of the garland had been written on, but it had obviously been done before the paper had been folded and snipped. But there were snippets of texts left on the paper that I could still make out. I picked out a few words I could read clearly: "you and me," "forever," and, strangely, the word "tattoo." Then, near the top of the cut-out umbrella, I found the phrase "not what I want."

And then the last line, the only one without any words snipped out of it, said this: "I won't tell anyone. Especially not Pa. Not until we have to."

My stomach plummeted. Wouldn't tell what? What secret were they sharing? And had it somehow lead to their big fight? To their separation? To the reason Aunt Grania chose to leave?

There was a clearly drawn circle too, near the bottom of the garland, partially snipped off, but it was half-shaded in with pencil, like a half-eaten pie, or diagram in a math book that designated the fraction 1/2.

What in the world was this supposed to mean? Was it a reference to their twin-ness? How they were each one half of a whole?

I stared at the back of that silhouette garland for a good, long while, and I wondered at my mother, at her sister, at their entire lifetime of sisterhood, in a way that I hadn't quite done before. Had they told their own inside jokes? Did they share friends and help each other with homework? Did they argue over whose turn it was to clean the litter box?

Had they been able to have an entire conversation with just the wrinkle of a nose or the raising of an eyebrow?

It was kind of a revelation. Of course. Mama and Grania must have been just like Tempest and me.

Until . . . what? Until they weren't anymore. And how had that happened?

I hung that red frame back on the pod wall, mulling it all over. What hadn't Mama told anyone? What would she not tell Pa?

Aunt Grania and Mama kept some kind of secret, stayed separated in their whole adult life, and Mama said it was *never her choice*. When I paired all that information with my mother's Sad Mama moments, I felt a growing uneasiness.

I quickly grabbed my stuff for the shower and took off out of our pod. The whole time I was shampooing my hair, I worried over Mama and Aunt Grania's secrets. And what was with that half-shaded circle? Was it some kind of code? Or more like a secret wink, an emoji, just some sign shared between the two of them?

I dressed quickly and hurried to find my sister.

Fat Sam called out his hellos from near the Spaceship 3000. "Have you seen Tempest?" I asked him.

"She's having breakfast with Molly-Mae."

"Thanks." I took off down the midway. I wanted to find Tempest, to tell her about what I'd found, whatever it meant. Maybe she'd help me look for more clues.

It seemed to me that if I could pinpoint what made Aunt Grania decide to leave Mama behind, then maybe, just maybe, I could keep Tempest from abandoning me.

When I got to the Candy Wagon, Tempest was there at the counter, eating an omelet, a tall glass of orange juice in front of her, Molly-Mae at the fryer.

"I could teach you bridge or pinochle," Molly-Mae was saying. "Or poker. We could have some fun betting." Molly-Mae was always jumping at the chance to spend more time with us, proposing all kinds of bonding moments. We could visit the new Sea Animal Sanctuary in Brunswick. She could teach us how to make stained glass. She could take us for tea at the King and Prince Hotel on St. Simons.

Molly-Mae was an excitable lady.

She and Tempest probably had big plans for the summer already. Heck, Tempest might have been writing her letters all year long, for all I knew.

Molly-Mae noticed me. "Oh, Tally! I'm making your favorite. Just give me a minute. The hash browns have to brown up."

"Glory, hallelujah!" I said. "I'm hungry." I took a seat next to my sister. "I nearly slept through teardown. Can't say that I'm sorry."

"Sounds about right," Tempest said.

"Listen, I gotta tell you something." I already had it all planned in my head. How we'd do some interrogations, sleuth out whatever secret thing had wedged its way between Mama and Aunt Grania, then we'd spend the rest of our carnival summer laughing about how we would never be so dramatic, our bond thick and strong again. It was a plot straight out of a Trenton Sisters Double-Special Holiday Mystery.

We'd get back to being inseparable again.

But just as I was about to tell Tempest, I noticed she wasn't just eating her breakfast. She was eating her breakfast with a teacup-sized, black-and-white kitten sitting in her lap. The kitten was all whiskers and ears with a tiny, pink nose. And the tip of her tail looked like it had been plopped into a can of white paint.

"Well, good morning!" I said, taking the kitten from Tempest and placing her in my lap.

Tempest's face went sour. "Tally, I was petting her!"

"Animals like me better," I said.

"Not always. Mary Anning used to hide your socks in her litter box," Tempest responded. Molly-Mae and I laughed at that. But my insides did a little twist. I didn't want to think about Mary Anning. I scratched the little kitten's neck and a purr rumbled in her throat.

"That's right. You named your cat after a scientist," Molly-Mae said.

Tempest nodded. "Yep. Mary Anning discovered the first dinosaur fossils."

"This one's name is Licorice," Molly-Mae offered, plopping a plate of hash browns in front of me. "Pa Charlie rescued her at our last stop, near Macon. He knows how much I love cats and, well, she's our new addition." She grabbed the frying pan and scooped up a few slices of bacon on her spatula, adding some to both our plates.

"So, how is Mary Anning?" Molly-Mae asked.

"She died," Tempest said.

"Oh! I'm sorry to hear that."

"These hash browns are my favorite thing on earth," I said to Molly-Mae, hoping to change the subject.

Tempest said, "Of course, Tally is never going to apologize for what happened with Mary Anning. Are you, Tally?"

Molly-Mae looked at me all open-mouthed.

"I didn't kill the cat. She was old and died," I said. "Jeez, Tempest. You make me sound so evil." I busied myself by scratching Licorice's belly.

"So you aren't apologizing?" Tempest asked.

"For what, exactly?" We'd been through this a dozen times.

I waited for Tempest to continue the argument, but she didn't.

I took a bite of bacon and offered my bacon-greased fingertips to Licorice to lick. "Does Mama have a tattoo?" I asked.

"What? No!" Tempest said. She eyed the kitten, who had jumped onto my shoulder and was biting at my ponytail. Tempest rolled her eyes. "You know? I need to go work on my . . . thing," she said. "Thanks for breakfast, Molly-Mae."

"Wait," I said, pulling the cat back into my lap.

"What?" Tempest asked.

I wanted to talk to my sister about what I'd found. I did. But looking at her pinched face, I stopped myself. She didn't want to spend her day interrogating the carnies about a few words scrawled on the back of Mama's paper chain. Tempest surely had some gadgets that needed building, an invention that needed a blueprint. Plus, she still hated me because of Mary Anning.

"What are you working on now, anyway?" I asked lamely.

"A liar gauge." Tempest shrugged like she couldn't be bothered to explain it.

Suddenly, I was tired of the work that it took to be interested in my sister. She turned to leave, and I let her.

I took Licorice out of my lap and placed her on the ground, where she immediately waged a battle against a roly-poly bug. She batted at it with her paw, then backed off, tail all puffed up, courage spent, until she found her druthers to attack it again.

I tried just to watch Licorice, and not to remember Mary Anning's death. Mary Anning had been an ugly cat with one milky, blind eye, and she used to love waging war on a cookie crumb or an errant grain of rice. She'd skitter across the kitchen floor after whatever she'd found like it was all that mattered to her in the world.

"You got a funny look on your face, Tally Jo," Molly-Mae said.

I didn't respond.

"You're not going to tell me what happened with the cat?"

I shrugged. I didn't want to tell Molly-Mae. It was too sad.

I'd found Mary Anning curled up next to the chicken coop, and I'd known right away she was nearing the end. Dr. Fran had warned us it was coming. So I scooped Mary Anning up and took her to Dr. Fran at the shelter. I stayed and comforted Mary Anning until she was gone, even though she'd never been my cat, really. I didn't go get Tempest. I didn't call her. I handled it myself.

Tempest had loved that cat so much, and I had sheltered her from the pain of watching her die.

Tempest didn't see it that way.

She was still mad at me about it. Blamed me for . . . whatever.

But when I thought of those last hours, of Mary Anning struggling for breath, the ugliness of it, the choking sadness of the whole thing, I was still glad Tempest didn't have to witness it.

Some things about this life were so bad, so god-awful, so final.

I knew Tempest was mad at me about it. Still.

But the thing was, I'd do it again.

8

I spent the morning trying to teach Licorice to shake and sit, to roll over and speak. It went about as well as teaching a pig to sing.

I was just wasting time, letting Tempest cool off. I planned on speaking to her on our way to St. Simons. It was always a long haul, traveling down the Georgia coast near into Florida. I'd have hours to get her on board with my sleuthing scheme, to make a plan for interrogating the carnies and getting to the bottom of why Aunt Grania left Mama.

But Tempest had other ideas. For the first time in the history of the universe, Tempest chose not to ride with Pa and me. Instead, she ducked into Molly-Mae's truck at the last minute, saying something about how Molly-Mae had a podcast on pie-baking they were dying to listen to.

Of course, Digger took the opportunity to jump into Pa Charlie's backseat with me and talk my ear off for four hours straight. I missed Tempest the whole time, and stared out the window wondering how we could ever get back to the old us. TallyandTempest. No spaces.

It was evening when our caravan of trailers, trucks, and motor homes pulled into the fairgrounds next to the scraggly little St. Simons Island Airport, which housed approximately two airplanes and a collection of antique kites.

I felt my heavy heart lift, just a little. St. Simons had always been one of my favorite stops with the carnival. Mama always called the downtown area, with all its old-fashioned buildings and its ancient lighthouse, "quaint" and "charming." Daddy said he loved it here because people hadn't quite learned to hurry up on St. Simons, because there wasn't any better place to go. We usually stayed near two weeks on the island, our longest stop of the summer.

The chore of setting up the carnival unfolded all around us, the scent of salt water in the evening air, the crunch of ground seashells mixed with the gravel on the midway.

I loved setup. There was just something about the silent, hopeful movements of the carnies as they unrolled canvas tents, bolted together the carousel and the rest of the rides, and created something nearly magical where there'd just been nothing. It was almost enough to jostle me from my grumpy mood, like maybe I could leave all my problems on the mainland. Like here on the island Tempest and I would be together and just fine again, getting along as easy as biscuits and gravy.

Like last summer. Like normal.

Tempest stuck to helping with the rides mainly, doing some of the smaller work, once the big pieces had been put into place, and I naturally secured the animals into their stalls. Digger did his main job, which was to talk. That hadn't changed.

Would I go with him to visit the Fort Frederica graveyard? Did I believe in ghosts?

Did I remember the year that we had climbed to the top of the lighthouse just as a lightning storm erupted over the sea?

Could we visit the shell shop down by the pier one day so he could mail a souvenir to his mother?

"Digger, don't you ever get tired of talking?"

"Tally, don't you ever get tired of crabbing?" He cracked himself up at that, laughing his Digger laugh.

I smiled even though I didn't want to. It was just that kind of day.

I found myself whistling Arnie's harmonica tunes as Digger pounded in the iron spikes to use as foundation for the swinging gates of the animal stalls. I held the spike for his first couple of hits without him even asking. We had done this quite enough to get it right. I did notice, however, that this year he only had to hit those stakes three, maybe four times. Not ten or eleven like last year, or like I'd probably have to do.

Digger wiped sweat from his brow, then asked, "What exactly is Tempest setting up to do?"

I turned to follow Digger's eyes. Sure enough, Tempest was talking with Pa Charlie, her hands waving through the air. I shrugged.

As Fat Sam dumped another pile of stakes in front of Digger, he answered, "I heard she's going to set up a booth."

I froze in place.

"Maybe for her gadgets?" Digger asked me.

I watched Fat Sam as he made his way back to setting up the Iron Witch, my mouth hanging open.

Tempest doing a booth? It was like a punch to the gut, hearing this news from anyone but Tempest herself. I felt Digger's eyes on me. So I tried to look like I didn't care.

Then Digger asked, "So what're you going to do?"

"What I always do," I answered, annoyed. "Work the animal booth."

"Jeez, Tally, keep your shorts on. I was just asking."

"It sounds like you're trying to say something." I gave him the best skunk eye I could.

"I would never do any such thing to Tally Trimble. I would never, ever take my life into my hands like that." He smirked then, and I could only smirk back.

Then he made his voice gentle. "What's happened between you and your sister?"

I sighed. So he'd noticed. "I don't know, Digger."

He kept talking. "It's just strange watching the two of you operate this year. Something's off, ya know? Like you're both dancing without a partner. Feels funny to have something between y'all."

"Will you just can it, Digger, all right?"

"Jeez, Tally. I was just saying. It's just what Fat Sam always said about you: you're like two halves of a whole, ya know?"

I couldn't look Digger in the eye then, because I didn't want him to see what that sentence did to me. It hurt me, like my breath had been stolen. I stood up and turned my back to Digger, busied myself studying my cuticles like they held the answers to the universe.

Tempest was setting up her own carnival booth? For what?

And if Digger could tell Tempest and me weren't ourselves, well, that made it feel true. It made it real.

It put a raw edge to my feelings, making them vulnerable and exposed.

How had this all happened?

Digger was right: I was without my other half. But that wasn't quite right, though, was it? I mean, Tempest was more than that to me, because two halves of a whole implied an easy separation, when really, it was much more complicated than that.

She was the butter on my toast, the sea to my shore, the stars in my night sky.

"You okay, Tally?"

"I'm fine, Digger Swanson. Give a girl a minute." I was just coming to terms with the fact that what used to be between Tempest and me had been as strong and as unbreakable as an iron girder, but now, what was between us? A cobweb maybe. Broken by a breeze, a look, a word.

I heard Digger's footsteps behind me and I tensed up, hoping he would have enough sense not to try and comfort me.

"Tally?" he said, standing right behind me, and for one terrible second I thought he was going to put his arm around me, and I didn't think I could take that. I couldn't take comfort from Digger Swanson. I had my pride.

"I'm fine, Digger."

"You sure?"

He moved a bit closer still.

It made me want to throw a tantrum like I used to when I was four years old. Just scream and yell and roll around on the ground.

"You know, it's tough, Tally Jo, when things go a-changing."

"Yeah." I hated the way my voice shook, and I wiped away one traitor tear that spilled down my cheek.

"When my parents divorced, Tally Jo," Digger said. "I got sadder than I think I ever been."

I turned to stare him down.

"I ain't sad, Digger."

"Okay." Digger raised his eyebrows at me.

"I'm not."

"Whatever you say, Tally Jo."

"I say I'm fine."

"Then you're fine."

I reached out and punched him right in the shoulder. He didn't even bring up his other hand to rub it.

"People who get all sad are just weaklings. I'm not a weakling."

Digger's face blanched, and I realized how I had put my foot in my mouth. "Hey, wait."

"Forget it." He turned to grab a bale of hay.

"Really, I didn't mean it. I just—"

"It's nothing, Tally, really." Digger ignored me and went about his chores.

Well, I'd certainly been a grade A slime to him. But why in the saltine cracker did he have to go prying like that?

I stamped off and grabbed Antique from his aluminum trailer. He neighed a low thanks when I let him out of that closed-in space. I led him along the midway to the tent, stroking his mane, and confiding my frustrations without saying a word. Like a good friend, he whinnied in commiseration. I petted Antique's nose, letting his presence comfort me. The sweet smell of fresh hay; the steady rise and fall of the horse's ribs with each breath; the slow blink of his dark, intelligent eyes; and the sweet nudge of his nose into my shoulder when I hugged him around his neck. Animals didn't need words.

Digger and I made quick and silent work of readying the rest of stalls. Then we led the animals into their areas, spread the fresh hay, watered them. I left to let the goats into their pens and grab Cokes for Digger and me.

When I came back, I found Digger lying in the wolf-pup stall, wrestling with them. "You're gonna smell like dog," I told him thoughtfully. I handed him his can of Coke.

"Probably better than what I usually smell like," he answered, letting one of the wolf pups bite on his raggedy hair. He pulled the tab off his Coke and drank a long pull. Then he waved his shirttail back and forth in front of another pup, tempting him into a game of tug-of-war. I opened the stall door and sat down with them, bringing the fourth pup into my lap and scratching him behind the ears. He had a gorgeous salt-and-pepper coat and the bluest eyes.

"Sometimes I wonder what it'd be like to know you during the school year, Tally," Digger said, letting one of the pups chew on his index finger. "Bet you would keep me in line."

"Nah, I'd be too cool for you," I joked.

"You still the student council president and all that?"

"Of course."

"Tempest still your vice president?"

"Nah."

"Well, I'm still a baseball stud."

"Right," I teased. "So you say. You and Pa named these guys yet?"

"Nah. We can't get too attached, Tally. Your grandpa says we won't be able to keep them after a few more weeks. They'll have to go to a shelter or something, maybe get reintroduced to the wild."

"They still need names, for crikey's sake."

"Pork Chop," Digger announced, pointing at the one snarling at his T-shirt, his muzzle low to the ground. He was smaller than the others, but fierce. The pup hopped up and attacked Digger in one smooth motion. Digger laughed his grumbly laugh and let the pup gnaw at his T-shirt, his fingers, the bottom of his Coke can.

The one that had been nipping Digger's hair had stopped and was nosing through the hay, sniffing at everything. "Sniffer," I proposed.

The pup in my lap had curled himself up into a furry ball. "Cuddles, of course." I scratched his ears, and he whimpered a little, moving his paws in his sleep.

The other pup just sort of sauntered around the corners of the stall, keeping his space from everyone. "What's that one like?" I asked.

"That one's always got her own ideas. She's the one that snuck out in Cranston. Found her nosing around with the goats, the goats shivering like there was no tomorrow. The pup just fell asleep up in their hay bale, but the goats nearly died of fright. She's an odd one."

I noticed she had a black spot on her forehead that the other pups did not. "It's a girl," Digger said. "I think we'll call her Tally." And with that he started laughing like there wasn't anything funnier in all the world. "She's a strange bird. So we'll call her Tally."

I got up and stomped right out of that stall, swinging the gate shut hard, with a loud clank. But I was smiling. Digger always got me, that was for sure. But I eyed the hose off to my left, and I grabbed that sucker and, let me tell you, Digger quit laughing pretty quick when I sprayed him down with some very cold water.

Then it was my turn to cackle.

9

With Tempest off doing her own thing, I realized with a sinking feeling that this stay in St. Simons was indeed not going to be like any other summer. Tempest was busy and distant, working on her own things. I found myself thinking of the silhouette garland in our pod: the two girls, nearly identical, but not.

I'd always known which girl I was: the one leaning into her sister, taking charge of the umbrella. That was me.

I was the leader, the protector. So I would solve this mystery myself, keep us together. And since Digger was always following me around anyway, I enrolled him as my assistant in the Greenly Twin Mystery.

I showed Digger the cut-out note on the back of the silhouette garland. He was thrilled, as Digger had no other mode of operation than one hundred percent enthusiasm.

So, on that first full day on the island, after doing our animal-tent chores, Digger and I got to work. We sat in my pod, a notebook in my lap, and we planned our sleuthing.

I explained, "Digger, we need to interrogate everybody. We gotta get them to tell us all they know about my mama and her sister."

"I'll use my charm."

"Right." I rolled my eyes. "We should make a list of people who could know things, starting with who's been here forever." I jotted down several names.

"We should start with Arnie the Carnie," Digger said.

"Why him? Folks like your dad and Pa Charlie have been here the longest."

"Well, we have to work our way up to interrogating the likes of Pa Charlie. And we need to get a feeling for how deep this secret is. That kind of thing. Plus, Arnie's got all those tattoos, and we know your mama wrote the word tattoo on there. Maybe he knows something."

It was about all we had to go on at this point. And I was impressed with Digger's logic. He took my pencil and put a check next to Arnie's name on our list.

Soon after, we sat in the trailer Arnie shared with Hames, watching him polish a long silver sword with a brown leather grip. When I asked Arnie to tell us what he knew of my mama and her sister, he quirked his eyebrow at me. A man of few words (and many, many mermaid tattoos), Arnie fixed me with a stare.

"What are you getting at, Tally Jo?" Arnie asked.

"They never came back here after their last year of high school, did they? Never together, right?"

"You think they had some kind of falling out, like all soap-opera dramatic?"

"I reckon they did. Do you know what it was about?"

He dipped a rag into a gray, putty-like substance and worked at a scuff on the curlicue engraving covering the sword's blade. He tilted his head like he was considering. Digger picked up another knife, a small one—maybe a dagger —on the low coffee table, and he dragged his finger lightly across the blade. "These could slice somebody's fingers off. You keep them shiny for the shows?"

Once in a while, usually over July 4th weekend, Pa Charlie would make concessions toward fireworks, and then we'd put on a whole special circusy kind of sideshow. Molly-Mae would pretend to tell fortunes, Hames would swallow fire and create balloon animals. And Arnie here would swallow enormous swords right down his gullet.

Arnie gave Digger a funny look. "It doesn't matter to me if the swords are shiny, but I do want them to be clean, Digger Swanson. When they're going down my very own throat, I don't need a boatload of germs." Arnie glared at Digger like he wasn't quite thinking right.

"You don't worry about slicing your neck open, but you worry about germs?"

"Of course," Arnie answered. "I'm not stupid."

Digger went to respond but thought better of it.

Arnie turned to me, "Why don't you ask Fat Sam or your pa about this, Tally? I don't think I can tell you much, even if I wanted to. The whole thing was before my tenure here. I've only known your mama and Grania separately."

"Have they ever asked you about tattoos?"

"Can't say that they did."

I looked at Arnie with narrowed eyes. Was he telling me the truth? I didn't have any choice but to think he was.

After I dragged Digger away from the swords, we tracked down Fat Sam, who was busy doing a test run of the newly renovated Iron Witch. The famous Tilt-a-Whirl was an attraction that a lot of carnival-goers loved. Little did they know that it was the most hated ride on the whole midway, at least from the workers' perspective, because it weighed an absolute ton, so repairing it, tearing it down, setting it up, all of it was serious work. And dangerous.

I saw a greenie get his left arm crushed under the weight of one of those pieces when I was about seven years old, and I still think about that when I see a mess of raw hamburger. It was not a pretty thing.

"You remember last time my Aunt Grania was here with my mama?" I asked Fat Sam.

"Oh, sure. Their last summer together was about the time we gave up the reptile show."

I didn't like that phrase. *Their last summer.*

"Peachtree had a reptile show?" Digger asked.

"Yes indeed. It was your mother's idea," Fat Sam told Digger. "She had a friend with a baby alligator." He waved his hand in the air, like, *What are you gonna do?*

"And, well, your mom and I took that little bugger in, raised him. Godzilla, of course, was his name. He grew right large, quickly thereafter." Fat Sam wrenched the lever of the Iron Witch forward, tilting his head like he was listening to something, maybe the chug and hum of the motor.

"A baby alligator?" Digger asked. "Why didn't I inherit him?"

"Got much too big. We had to donate him to an outfit in Tallahassee. Alligator wrestling and such."

The Iron Witch clinked and clanked its rhythm now, turning in circles, going faster and faster. Fat Sam studied its motion, his brow furrowing.

"You think the Iron Witch has another summer in her?" I asked.

"That is the question, Miss Tally," Fat Sam said, his eyes flitting to Digger, who was strangely quiet.

Digger's eyes had glazed over. He was remembering things. A different time, when he had both his parents together, maybe?

Or dreaming of having a mammoth reptile as a brother. You never knew with Digger.

"Your mom and I were just talking about that summer on the phone," Fat Sam said to Digger.

"You talked to Mom on the phone?"

"Sure," Fat Sam said.

Digger turned and waggled his eyebrows at me like this was the greatest news on earth. Probably he was dreaming of their reconciliation, but I didn't have time for Digger's family drama. I needed information.

"So what can you tell us about Grania?" I asked.

Fat Sam smiled. "Well, I've been working here since I was a kid. Your mother and Grania and I used to get into our fair share of scrapes and trouble." He laughed, sounding just like Digger.

"What was Aunt Grania like?" I asked.

He pulled the lever into the stop mode for the Iron Witch and tapped at his bottom lip. "Well, Grania was very daring. Always putting me up to something. And fun. Like your mother, but louder. Your mother always had her nose in a book, but Grania liked other people's business better." He smiled, but then it was like he caught himself. Suddenly, his smile was gone. "I'm not supposed to be talking to you about this."

I narrowed my eyes. "Why?"

"Pa Charlie's orders."

Digger's wide eyes met mine.

Now we were really on to something. So it wasn't my imagination that there were secrets at work here. Big secrets.

"Please. I gotta know, Fat Sam."

"Look, I don't have the real nitty-gritty details, Miss Tally, but I—"

Digger interrupted, "It's her family, Dad. You need to help her out."

"Can't you give me hint or even—"

Fat Sam held up his hand. "Hold your horses, kids. Tell you what, you two do me a favor, and I will think about it. I might have some information for you. I could tell you at least the snippets I know."

"Really?" I asked.

"That sound like a deal?"

I caught Digger's eye. We both said it at once: "Deal."

10

That's how Digger and I found ourselves cleaning out the catch-all on a sweltering June day, sweating half to death and grumbling under our breath. The catch-all was what everybody at Peachtree called this old, ratty, rusted-out box trailer that Molly-Mae towed behind her truck for no apparent reason, aside from the fact that everybody threw anything extra into it. If something was of no apparent use, but maybe would be someday, for this or that, it went in. If we were being honest, everybody knew it was mostly trash.

But, oh, why don't we just throw it in the catch-all anyway, so Tally can clean it out in ninety-seven degree weather?

For example, did you need a papier-mâché strawberry the size of Digger's head that used to hang from the Candy Wagon menu board?

How about a grown-up-sized kangaroo costume, complete with stuffed-animal joey in the pouch?

Or stacks of old, washed-out Peachtree banners, flyers, and road signs?

What about six pink plastic flamingos?

"When did Peachtree have clowns?" I asked, reaching into a tattered cardboard box that used to hold a Christmas tree. I pulled out a pair of oversized red shoes, rainbow-striped overalls, and several crayon-bright wigs. I tried on a pair of round spectacles with lenses the size of dinner plates.

I looked over toward the old oak tree, the lenses of the glasses making everything look sort of wavy. I could see Licorice under the tree, curled up on Pa Charlie's old blue-and-green quilt.

Digger stuck on a red clown nose. "I don't know why we ever got rid of clowns, but we should have them again immediately." He discovered a brass horn and squeaked it right in my ear.

"Digger Samuel Swanson!" I cried. I looked around us, and I blew the hair off my forehead. We had emptied the entire contents of the catch-all onto the patchy grass of the midway next to it. "We're supposed to be cleaning."

"We're *organizing*." He had the clown shoes on now, and his feet hit the ground with a delicious slapping sound with each step. "There are different stages of organizing. This first stage is called perusing. We're perusing the goods." He walked around the contents of the catch-all like a penguin and donned a powder-blue tuxedo jacket with more ruffles than I could count. I tried not to laugh. I pulled on a neon pink wig and dug into the box for more props.

"Holy kudzu," I said when my hands brushed something promising. It took me a few pulls, but I eventually got it out from the heap of clown clothes.

"What is it?"

"Meet my new best friend."

"A unicycle?" Digger laughed.

It was kind of rusty and looked like it needed air in the tire. The seat was cracked and ancient, but it was a beauty. "Oh yeah," I said, and I hopped on top of it. It took me a few tries to get my balance right and begin to pedal. But on the third try, I thought I had it. I pedaled a few feet across the gravel midway, but then I wiped out, flying forward, landing on my knees.

"It's so easy though!" Digger teased, laughing.

"Shut it, Swanson." But I was laughing too.

"Let me have a try."

I handed it over, and of course Digger was off like a shot, giant clown shoes and all. "Like riding a bike," he called.

"Of course. Very funny."

"Tally Jo?" I heard Pa Charlie call out. He was coming down the midway, walking toward us with Fat Sam. They made a funny silhouette against the horizon, Fat Sam as thin as a rail, Pa Charlie as round as Santa Claus.

"Yes sir?" I answered, walking to meet them.

"Nice work, Digger," Pa Charlie called, as Digger was flying all over on that unicycle. Darn him and his athletic abilities.

But I saw that Pa Charlie's brow was pinched, and his eyes scanned the mess we'd made in front of the catch-all.

"Oh, I promise we're cleaning up before the carnival opens tonight. I was going to—"

"That's fine. I know you will." He rubbed at his beard then. "Heard you been asking everyone about what happened between your mother and your aunt?"

My stomach dropped. I didn't like the disapproving look in Pa Charlie's eyes. I answered honestly, "Yes sir."

Digger had come up at my side then, balancing on the unicycle, and I watched his eyes snap to Fat Sam. "Don't look at me like that, son," Fat Sam said. "I just thought that Miss Tally should hear things from her Pa, and, well . . ." Fat Sam looked abashed.

I almost would've felt sorry for him, if I wasn't so darn aggravated.

Pa Charlie walked over to the nearest picnic table, his steps heavy and slow. Pa Charlie didn't often seem serious, even less often did he seem downtrodden. Right now, he seemed both.

"Come on over and let's have ourselves a little talk, Tally."

I watched Digger and Fat Sam exchange a look. Fat Sam motioned for Digger to move along with him. Digger lolly-gagged for a few seconds, but then he and Fat Sam left Pa and me to argue by our own selves.

I sat down across from him. I swallowed hard and worried my knuckles over my chin, staring at my pa.

He was nodding to himself like he was considering something.

He was going to tell me. Here it was.

I did feel a pinch of guilt for upsetting him. I did. But I was really going to learn what had happened with my aunt and my mother. I felt hot all over. I would finally know, so I could somehow stop it from coming between my sister and me. I could get my Tempest back.

"Where's your sister?" Pa asked.

"Apparently, working on her booth." I tried hard not to roll my eyes. I didn't completely succeed.

"Oh, right," Pa Charlie said. "Well, Tally, I've got something here for you." He set it on the picnic table and pushed it toward me. It was a photograph of Mama and Aunt Grania, back when they were kids. They looked a little older than us, probably high school age. They stood on opposite sides of a small stage, each holding one end of a long, beautiful silhouette garland. I stared at it for a moment.

We'd seen pictures of them before. Not many. But we had.

It was easy to tell Mama from Aunt Grania. Mama was Mama, and Aunt Grania was almost Mama, but not quite. Aunt Grania had sharper edges, a more furrowed brow. Staring at the photo, it made me miss Mama and Daddy.

Pa Charlie broke into my thoughts, "This was their act."

"Okay."

"Your mother and Grania used to take suggestions from the audience, kids usually, and then they would make a silhouette of whatever they were asked to—porcupines kissing, race cars rounding a corner, anything at all."

"They did this together?"

"Yes. It was something. They would fold up the paper together, and then they would both just start snipping away, each with a pair of scissors in their hand. They wouldn't talk, wouldn't plan."

"Wait, they did one garland together, at the same time?"

"Yes."

"They didn't draw the pattern onto the paper or anything?"

"Nope. Just started snipping away."

"That seems near impossible. I always thought Mama did this alone. I mean, how would they know where one should stop cutting and the other should start, if they were working at the same time, on the same piece of paper?"

Pa Charlie shrugged. "That is the question. Your granny used to say they were talking in their minds. That always left me a bit bumfuzzled."

My mind raced. Mama and Aunt Grania had something between them too. I bet they couldn't play hide-and-go-seek either. I bet they were like Tempest and me. Of course they were.

You'd think Mama would've said a lot of stuff like that growing up, comparing us to her and her sister. But, no. She didn't. It was weird, now that I stopped to consider it.

And all of a sudden I had a memory, out of nowhere, staring at the photograph of Mama and Aunt Grania. "Me and Tempest did something like that," I told Pa Charlie. "A long time ago."

"Did you now?"

"Tempest and I, I mean," I said, correcting my grammar, as Mama surely would want me to. "We could sit at the computer and type emails to our friends, me using the right hand side of the keyboard, Tempest the left. We would just somehow know what word we were supposed to be typing, what came next. Honestly, we'd never miss a beat."

"Yes, that does sound quite near impossible, Tally."

"We didn't talk, just went ahead and typed," I said to Pa Charlie. "We just worked that typing like we were one brain, one person."

"Well," Pa Charlie said, and he made a move to get up from the picnic table, like we had settled something, like this conversation was over. "I need to go see what's got the Iron Witch going so plinkety-plunkety." He turned to leave.

"Hey, wait!" I told him, grabbing his hand. "You have to tell me about them, Pa. Why aren't they friends still?"

"Friends? They're friends."

I rolled my eyes. "Not really, and you darn well know it. We've never even met her. What did they fight about? What came between them?" I felt a stab of pain in my chest when I thought of the words my mama had scribbled on the back of that silhouette garland: *you and me, forever.* Whatever she'd been writing about, the words had a desperate ring to them.

"Please, Pa Charlie," I begged. "Just tell me."

Pa Charlie ran a hand over his face, scrubbing at his whiskers, and he let out a monster of a sigh. "Your mama will be here in a couple weeks. She's the one to answer all of these questions, Tally. No one else." There was a gruff edge to Pa Charlie's usually honey-smooth voice, and I knew it was there to dissuade me.

But I didn't let it.

"Well, I'll just call Mama right now then." I stuck my chin out in a defiant way, and held my hand out to him, palm up. "Could I please use your phone?"

"Fine," he said, digging in his pocket and producing his cell phone. "But she's going to tell you the same thing I'm about to say. And I want you to listen. I want you to really hear me, young lady." That gruff edge in his voice had turned fully serious now, so I pushed aside my righteous anger for a second, and I looked him in the eye. I tried to really listen.

But it was hard, because his eyes surprised me. There wasn't anger there, and he wasn't annoyed like I expected. No, Pa Charlie's eyes looked sad. They were tender and raw, not the dancing eyes I was so used to. That sadness sapped some of my frustration.

I steeled myself. "Go on then, sir. What is it you want to tell me?"

He put a meaty paw over my hand on the table. His voice was low and rumbly. "Enjoy your summer, Tally Jo. Enjoy this time with your sister. With your aunt, with the rest of us here at Peachtree."

There was nothing sinister in that advice, nothing at all. But then why did it somehow feel like a threat?

Why is it so important that I enjoy this time? I wanted to scream. *Are we running out of time?*

But Pa looked so old right then. With his age-spotted bald head and the deep creases in his jowls, he looked like he always looked—like, normal old. But today, there was more to it, just something in his movements. They were weighed down with memories, and his eyes were full of some kind of secret anguish.

So I bit my tongue. I handed him back his cell phone.

I would wait for my mother to get here.

This wasn't like me. I wanted to shake something, or someone. I wanted to scream and yell and whine about things not being fair. But I was realizing something: when I had been looking at the photo of my mama and aunt, Pa Charlie hadn't looked at all. He'd purposefully looked away, studying the piles of garbage we'd made from the catch-all.

Maybe that photo . . . maybe seeing his daughters together . . . maybe it hurt him.

Maybe Aunt Grania and Mama's blowup, their distance from each other, maybe it wasn't just hurting Mama. It hurt Pa Charlie too. This thing with Aunt Grania and Mama, whatever was at the source of it, it had started between them, sure. But it had grown bigger than that and had darn near strangled the happiness right out of my Pa Charlie's eyes.

So instead of railing against all that was unfair in the world, instead of quizzing him on my mama, I gave my grandfather a break. "Pa Charlie, could you tell me what our grandmother was like?"

He gave me a surprised look, all lifted eyebrows, but then he stroked his beard a bit in thought, a smile playing at his lips. "She was a lot like you, Tally Jo." He got this kind of far-off look in his eyes. "Didn't let me ever win an argument, but, lawdy, it was fun to try with her." He stopped then, considering, as if he wasn't sure he should go on. "I started this carnival because of her."

"I never knew that."

"It started as a dare. She dared me to start up Peachtree, because she knew it was my dream. I used to work as a hog butcher. Did you know that?"

I shook my head.

"It was hard, grueling work. Bore down on me too, year after year. Well, your granny, she used to tell me, 'There's one thing standing between you and your heart's desire, and that one thing is fear.'" Pa Charlie harrumphed, his eyes looking faraway. "She was fearless. Just like you, Tally Jo."

"So, she gave you the nudge you needed to start up Peachtree?"

"She sure did. And now I get to travel this great country, with my dearest family, and we have the privilege of doling out a few magical memories to the good working people in small-town America."

"Well, Peachtree certainly does that, and—"

"Your granny's probably why I keep the dratted Iron Witch around," he went on, "even though it's darn near ready for the boneyard. Your granny loved that ride."

"Did she?" I smiled, trying to picture that.

"I'm getting nostalgic, Tally Jo. Never a good thing." He chuckled and pinned me with his eyes. "You know she had a twin sister too."

I nodded, wanting him to go on. "So many generations of twin girls," he said. "'The Greenly Curse of too many beautiful women,' your granny said when she gave birth to your mama and Grania." He laughed then, his belly jiggling, his shoulders shaking. "Your grandmother was a handy kind of gal. She hand-stitched all of her own clothes. Mine too, as a matter of fact. That quilt you had on you at the campfire, she made that with her sister. They both quilted and knitted. Right talented, they were. They used to mail each other half-finished quilts, when they lived halfway across the country from each other. They'd start the pattern themselves and then send it to the other one to finish it," Pa Charlie finished. His eyes slid away from me suddenly, and he coughed into his hand.

"Pa, your lunch is ready!" Molly-Mae called from the Candy Wagon.

Pa Charlie's enormous middle growled a symphony then, as if on cue, and we both chuckled.

There was that dancing jig, back in his eyes again. I smiled.

"Go on," I said. "Eat your lunch. I've got an entire catch-all to clean up." I motioned to our mess. "And . . . by the way, I like thinking I am a little like Granny. I barely remember her."

"Thanks for letting me talk about her." Pa Charlie got up from the table, rubbing at the small of his back.

"Thanks for the photo, Pa."

On his way to the Candy Wagon, Pa Charlie pointed to the quilt under the old oak. Licorice was still sleeping there, curled up with her nose tucked under her paws. "You should pick up the quilt, Tally. Don't let it get filthy on the ground. It's too precious to me."

"Yes sir," I said, looking at Granny's quilt with new eyes. I walked over to it, and picked it up, dislodging a none-too-happy Licorice, who attacked my ankles in retribution. I shook out the quilt and began to fold it.

Granny and her sister had made this, sending it back and forth, adding panels. Had they gone back and forth with it several times? One panel at a time, or more than that?

They had lived far away from each other. What had Pa said? Halfway across the country.

Separated.

Hmm.

I looked at the quilt more closely. Its geometric pattern had always seemed haphazard—the squares and hexagons, the little yellow triangles, all of it similar in each panel, but still a little different, no real rhyme or reason.

But now I looked again—really looked. Each panel had a blue background made from squares of different calico patterns: flowers, curlicues, swirls, but all in shades of blue. Then, there were smaller yellow triangles mixed in intermittently. But the real star of each panel was the green shape. It was often in the center of the panel, but sometimes not.

Then it hit me.

These panels were not just geometric shapes.

This quilt was not abstract and random. Not at all.

The green shape of each panel was a hexagon, not a circle, so maybe that's why I'd never made the leap before. But now—now I could see it so plainly, it made me wonder how in the jelly sandwich I hadn't seen it before.

The appliquéd hexagon, with its six sides, looked almost like a circle, but not quite. The first one started completely made of patches of light-green material. In the next panel it was the same, except a small sliver of the right side was made in darker green. As the panels went on, that dark green edged over the whole of the shape, overtook the entire hexagon, bit by bit. Like a circle getting shaded in, in small increments.

I stared at the quilt for a good long time, barely registering Digger out of the corner of my eye pedaling into view on the unicycle. It's like I was seeing its design for the first time. I mean, I'd snuggled into this quilt approximately seven million times. Slept under it, used it as a picnic blanket and as the roof of a card-table fort. I'd even thrown up on it once when I was seven, after a particularly rough ride on the Iron Witch, and there was a small, patched-up tear on the underside where I'd caught it on a chain-link fence near Macon.

This quilt had been around forever. But now, I truly saw it for what it was.

"Digger!" I called, "Come look!"

I spread the quilt out on top of the picnic table now, ran my fingertips across the fancy cross-stitching around the hexagon appliqués. "What do you see?" I asked him.

"What am I supposed to see?"

"That right there." I pointed to the hexagon in the first panel.

"Look," I told him. "What do you see, if you pay attention to the progression?" I pointed to the second panel of the quilt, then the third. Then I led him down to the second row, as if reading text on a page.

"Huh," Digger said.

"Yeah."

"That's a gosh-darn moon, Tally Jo."

The moon. It was clear as day.

"The quilt shows the phases of the moon," I said, my mind boggled. "This here quilt is telling a story, from a sliver of a moon to the full moon."

"This is a clue, Tally. Seriously," Digger said. "It's gotta be. This shape matches the one in the note on the back of the silhouette." Digger pointed. "That same shape. Think that's a moon too?"

"Yeah."

Licorice was now chewing a corner of the quilt and wrangling it between her teeth like it had just insulted her mother. "Shoo," I said, pulling her off. "So Mama and Grania fought over . . . the moon? A tattoo of the moon?"

"There's more to it," Digger said. "Everyone's acting so tight-lipped. There's gotta be more. This is big. Like . . . Godzilla big."

"My granny made this quilt with her sister. Her twin. There's history here." I felt a chill rush down the nape of my neck, as I rubbed the fabric between my fingers. "I think you could be right, Digger." We were getting close to something. We really were.

Licorice tried for the quilt again, so I picked her up and placed her on my shoulder. She hopped onto Digger's instead. She bit his earlobe and jumped down to the ground. Digger didn't even notice, his brow knit over the quilt, studying it. He tapped at his bottom lip with his forefinger.

"Hold up, I think I see steam coming out your ears. Don't overdo it." I chuckled then, but it was like Digger didn't hear me.

"The quilt is going from nothing to the full moon, right?" He pointed at the panels, and, for once, Digger didn't joke.

I got serious real quick. "Yeah? What are you thinking?"

Digger continued, "You know, a long time ago, farmers, and probably other people too, told time by the moon."

"Okay, yeah, so this is like a calendar?"

"Or almost like a . . . countdown."

"A countdown?"

"Yeah, maybe from new moon to the full moon," Digger guessed.

"That could be." A shiver went down the back of my neck again. "You still got your old phone, Digger?"

"Yeah." He produced it from his pocket.

"When's the next full moon?" I pictured the moon from last night. It had been a half-moon, or something close to it, golden and shining in the sky. The stars had been brighter than I was used to too. On St. Simons Island, everything seemed to shine a bit brighter.

Digger tapped some things on the screen of his phone. "The moon will next be full on the thirteenth of this month. That's next week. Maybe y'all are fixing to turn into werewolves or some such."

"Stop, Digger. Be serious."

"Right. Serious." He gave me some kind of ridiculous salute. "Hey, your birthday is the thirteenth."

"Yep. Our golden birthday."

Digger was still looking at his phone. "It's a Flower Moon this time, it says. Whatever that means."

"A Flower Moon?" I said.

"A kind of supermoon, when it's extra big in the sky for whatever reason. And really weird things happen at the Flower Moon." Digger laughed. "It says here the lambs born during the Flower Moon are almost always twins. The crops are always bumper, which I think means extra good. And babies born are mostly left-handed. Huh."

Suddenly, a heavy feeling constricted my chest. This was no coincidence. At all.

I pulled a breath into my lungs and they squeaked back at me.

The next full moon was on our birthday.

The Flower Moon, whatever that was. And I couldn't explain why—I didn't have words for it—but looking at my granny's quilt, I understood that this was telling me her story, my mama's story, and my story too.

I didn't yet know what that was.

But I knew it was something big.

11

That evening on St. Simons Island began in a blur of flashing carnival lights and cotton-candy clouds—a gorgeous clear night, perfect weather for a carnival, and the crowd size reflected that. The crowd surged with the sunset, the lights of the midway attracting the carnival-goers like moths to a flame. They came in waves, starting with the kids about our age, loud and laughing, spending most of their time at the games: throwing darts at balloons, trying to knock the milk bottles down, and shooting water guns at animated targets.

As the moon rose—edging toward three-quarters now—and the night settled in, more families showed up: harried-looking parents, squealing children, and lots of weekend cash. The petting zoo was a hit, and the kids especially loved our pups. We took in dollar after dollar inside the animal tent. First we charged a dollar for admission. Then we asked two bucks for a Ziploc baggie full of feed, and an extra fifty cents for a Milk-Bone if they wanted to feed the wolf pups. And we darn near ran out of both. Kids were right happy to get down and dirty with the animals. Pork Chop seemed to be in a mood. He even bit one kid who tried to pet him, but it wasn't so bad. I bribed the boy quiet with a monstrous cloud of cotton candy.

Like Pork Chop, I was agitated throughout the evening, hoping for a quiet moment when I could go find my sister and her newfangled booth. When, a little before eleven, the crowd in the animal tent finally began to wane, Digger and I sneaked out toward the midway, scanning the carnival for Tempest.

I spotted her right away. She sat next to the strongman bell, not in a booth exactly, just at this rickety card table. She wasn't one for fanfare. She had her usual gears and springs spread out in front of her, with some kind of makeshift sign taped up.

Tempest: always a little left-of-center.

"Come on," I said. Digger looked about as worn-out as I felt, with hayseeds caught in his hair and a small gash on his cheek from a run-in with one of the ill-tempered turkeys.

A couple of high schoolers were just leaving Tempest's booth, shaking their heads, as we approached. The boy pulled on his baseball hat in a nervous fashion. "I can't believe that chick. She knew my cell phone number. Well, most of it. That can't be safe, can it?"

Digger raised his eyebrows. "How is she rigging this?"

I peered at Tempest's makeshift booth. I shrugged, feeling that odd mix of irritation and worry toward Tempest as we approached her table. I registered a low-level thrum. That pressure was alive again between us. My heart sank. It was back—not bad, but enough. It made my teeth ache.

I kept a safe distance.

Tempest's sign—hand-printed in purple marker—was all sorts of vague. It read I'LL GUESS YOUR NUMBER FOR A QUARTER.

"Okay," Digger said. "That doesn't make much sense."

"No, it doesn't." *But it's Tempest*, I added in my mind. And that meant it did make some kind of sense to me. Numbers—she'd always been good with numbers. They went hand in hand with her doodads.

A Kool-Aid-mustached kid plopped his quarter down on the table in front of Tempest. Tempest eyed him up and down. Then she gave Digger and me a little wave. She had a weird gadget in her hands: what looked like a rejiggered compass, bearing the face of a tire pressure gauge, with three tiny, silver antennae sticking out of one edge. She fiddled with it nervously.

I guessed it was her liar gauge.

"Twenty-seven," she announced firmly.

"That don't mean nothing to me," the boy said, licking at his chapped red lips. I kind of wanted to yank on his ear, correct his grammar.

"Think harder. It does." Tempest's voice was so confident. She blinked hard only once.

The boy's brow furrowed and he brought his finger up to his temple in a gesture of deep thought. Digger elbowed me, grinning, and this whole scene was just about to make me laugh out loud too. Except that it scared me a bit. What in the peanut butter and bananas was Tempest doing?

And why did I feel like it was pulling her farther away from me?

Suddenly, the boy's eyes popped open. "You're right!" He smiled brightly. "I can't scarce believe it, but you're right!" He turned on his heel then, and he took off toward the Candy Wagon.

"Wait!" Digger and I called in unison. The boy turned back around.

"What was twenty-seven?"

"I won a cupcake-eating contest last month in my Cub Scout troop. I ate twenty-seven of them. Got myself a trophy."

Digger's eyes met mine and we busted out laughing at the absurdity of it all. Tempest cleared her throat. "Excuse me," she said. "I'm trying to run my booth here."

She had her chin stuck out at an odd angle, like we'd some-how hurt her feelings. "How do you do this?" I asked her. "Is it just some kind of lucky guess or is it—"

"Magic?" she finished for me.

I nodded. Tempest shrugged. "It's science before it's explained, that's all." Then she went on, quieter, like maybe she shouldn't. "Tally, you've got something too, you know."

"What? No I don't."

"You do; you're just scared."

"Tempest, stop it, okay?"

"Okay," said Tempest in a way that made it quite clear that it was indeed *not* okay.

"Okay," I agreed, trying to end this conversation, my throat pinching tight. I didn't *have* anything. And I didn't *want* anything, either, if it meant that I was going to be like Tempest, completely absorbed in my own inventions, forgetting about my one true friend.

A round-faced girl with a mess of red curls slapped her quarter down on Tempest's table. "What if I tell you that you're wrong, even though you guess it right? Then what?" she asked with a sneer.

Tempest just shrugged. "I'll know. I can tell if you're lying." She fingered the gadget on the table.

The girl gave Tempest a scowl but handed over her quarter. Tempest ran her eyes up and down the girl, considering.

"I see the number ten and the number twenty."

The girl pursed her lips. Then her eyes widened and she said, "It's my birthday. Tenth month of the year—October—twentieth."

Tempest gave her an I-told-you-so look and the girl walked away in a huff.

"Seriously. Whoa," Digger said. "How do you—"

"I don't know yet. I can't explain it."

"It's gotta be some kind of trick, doesn't it?" Digger offered. "Some kind of guess with odds and—"

But I knew it wasn't a trick. And it didn't really have any-thing to do with her gadgets. Tempest had something, plain and simple.

It was real.

What Tempest was doing . . . it was something akin to magic. Not unlike what we used to have between us, how we couldn't play hide-and-go-seek, how we sometimes knew what the other was thinking. That kind of thing, but bigger, stronger, scarier.

Not exactly controllable.

Like the strange pressure that uncoiled and bloomed between us now, erupting here and there with no warning. Waxing and waning with no real pattern to it.

Yes. Just like that.

Right then I heard a voice, and although I was still focused on Tempest's liar gauge, there was something familiar about it. It tickled at the back of my mind. "I have a quarter."

"Tally," Digger said.

"What is it?" I said, watching the liar gauge, trying to figure out how in the creamed corn it worked.

"Tally," Digger said again, and now he was yanking on my elbow too.

And when I looked up I understood. Because there stand-ing in front of a stunned Tempest was Grania Greenly.

It was the oddest feeling, seeing this woman standing there. It was Mama, but not Mama. She carried a leather bag, stuffed to the gills. She wore a long, flowery skirt, and bracelets, tons of them. All silver and jangling on her left wrist.

There were so many weird, déjà vu sensations coming at me at once that I could barely process any of it. "Holy pea-pods," I whispered.

"Here's my quarter, but I really only want a hug," she said with a smile, pressing her coin to Tempest's card table. "Surprise! It's Tempest? Am I right?"

Tempest nodded, her knuckles white around the liar gauge.

There were teachers who had known us for years and couldn't tell us apart. Marisol even got it wrong sometimes, if she wasn't paying close attention. And Aunt Grania knew?

Aunt Grania pulled Tempest into a hug and kissed both of her cheeks with a flourish. Next, she turned and did the same to me, and I took in her scent. "My girls!" she said. "I feel like I know you! It is so wonderful to finally meet you in person."

As much as she looked like Mama, moved like Mama, sounded like Mama, she didn't smell like her. Mama always wore the same perfume—she smelled like baby powder and roses. Aunt Grania smelled like some kind of spice and freshly-cut grass. I thought then, for some reason, of that day when Tempest and I had done our fingerprints.

"It's nice to meet you," Tempest stammered.

"You don't have any gray hair," I blurted. Mama had some. Surely Aunt Grania should.

"Magnets," she said. "They're useful for all kinds of things."

"Thirteen," Tempest said.

"That's my number?" Aunt Grania asked, a smile playing around her mouth.

Tempest nodded again, looking totally stricken, and my eyes shot to Digger.

"Tempest, you okay?" Digger asked her.

She nodded, still looking at Aunt Grania. "Am I right?"

"Hmm," Aunt Grania said. "Let me think. I don't know if that makes any sense for me. Nope, I can't seem to place that one."

Tempest's cheeks flamed red.

Thirteen.

I knew why it was her number. I might not know much, but I was starting to put some pieces together. Digger and I had Googled a whole heap of things about the lunar cycle, learning details about the moon and its phases.

"Thirteen moons," I said. "That's how many moons from sliver to full moon. Thirteen."

"What are you talking about?" Tempest asked.

Aunt Grania stood frozen and silent, her easy friendliness slipping. Maybe she hadn't known she'd be walking into an interrogation.

"What do the moons mean? What does it have to do with why you and Mama don't see each other anymore?"

"Tally," Digger warned.

"No, I don't see why we have to dance around everything. Digger and I figured out the quilt—Granny's quilt. It tells the story of the moon. And the full moon's coming on our birthday.

And somehow that's connected to you and Mama. What does it all mean?"

Aunt Grania had recovered somewhat now, and she smiled. "Oh, yes, June thirteenth? Your golden birthday, correct? Are we doing anything special here at the carnival?"

Her small talk was a weak, half-hearted attempt to avoid answering my questions, and I wasn't having it. "The moons are counting down to something, I know it. But what?"

In a very un-Mama-like way, Aunt Grania grimaced. She put her hand on her hip. "Tally, I just got here. I am sensing a lot of aggression in you, and to be quite honest, I don't have any idea what you're talking about."

Tempest dropped the liar gauge on the rickety card table. It was ticking something fierce, clicking and clacking, its antennae moving briskly from side to side.

"What in the saltine cracker?" I said, but I wasn't looking at the liar gauge anymore. I'd spied something else.

I pointed right at Aunt Grania's arm, where the phases of the moon played out in a circle around her wrist. I didn't have time to count the moons before she snatched her arm from view, pressing it to her middle and covering it with her other hand, but I would bet on Bones's life there were thirteen. "Tell me why you have thirteen moons tattooed on your wrist."

"A warning," she said, but then it was like she realized she shouldn't be speaking. Aunt Grania shook her head.

Tempest seemed to find her voice. "Tally, you found all this stuff out and you didn't tell me?"

"I wanted to. I was going to."

"When?"

"Soon." I knew I needed to talk to Tempest. I did. But I wasn't ready to let this go with Aunt Grania. I was so incredibly close. I had to push. I bore my eyes into hers. "Why did you leave my mama?" *How could you be so heartless?*

She shook her head. "That's what you think happened? That's your hypothesis?" She laughed then—this ugly, bitter sound. "My dear, I'm afraid you don't have a clue what you're talking about."

"Grania Greenly!" It was Pa Charlie's honey-soft voice, calling from near the bonfire. A riot of greetings erupted from the rest of the carnival workers.

"Dad!" Aunt Grania called, waving her arm over her head, her bracelets jangling down to her elbow. She moved toward the bonfire, surely ecstatic to get away from us. Aunt Grania turned over her shoulder. "We'll talk later," she said.

Later would probably be never, if she had her way.

My body was fairly thrumming with something—anticipation, dread, a combination of both.

I moved to follow Aunt Grania.

Tempest reached out to grab my elbow, but she stopped herself. I could feel why—it was there again, between us, blooming bigger. But Tempest gave it no notice as she laid into me. "I can't believe you, Tally Jo, jumping all over her the second she appears at Peachtree and—"

"I'm trying to keep us from ending up like them."

"Like I'm not?" She picked up her liar gauge, shoving all her trinkets in her pockets. "All this stuff I'm doing, it's for us!"

"Oh, fat lot of good it's doing us. I could've told you Aunt Grania was lying. I didn't need a gauge for that." My mood darkened like a thundercloud.

"Not just this thing, Tally. But my other invention too. The tides, the magnets . . . it's all about us! You know what? Forget it." She stormed off toward the campfire, and I let her go.

Digger started up, "You know—"

"Can it, Digger," I told him.

"Got it, Tally Jo. I think I'm just gonna make myself scarce."

"You do that."

"Tally!" Pa's voice carried over to me, and it was sharp. "Get over here." I didn't dare disobey him, so I trudged over to the campfire, and Pa Charlie had his arm around Molly-Mae, whose cheeks were pinker than usual.

His eyes searched mine, but then he looked away with a sigh, seeming to work hard to find his smile. Then Pa Charlie cleared his throat. "We're making some changes to our schedule this year, y'all, and with Grania here now, I thought we'd let the cat out of the bag."

Digger elbowed me. I scowled at him. Like I was supposed to care about this right now?

"Girls," he said, looking over at me, and then back at my sister. His true smile lit his face. "Molly-Mae and I were wondering something. Would you mind terribly much sharing your birthday celebration this year?"

"We're having a celebration?" Tempest asked.

"I've already been working on the cake," Molly-Mae said, smiling. "It'll be a right party. Your parents will be here by then."

"Will you be here still?" Tempest asked Aunt Grania.

Aunt Grania shook her head once, then said, "Pa Charlie, what exactly are you planning to do along with the girls' birthday party?"

Pa Charlie beamed. "Molly-Mae has done me the honor of accepting my proposal. We were thinking of getting hitched at the little seaside chapel in Ambersville, then having a wedding celebration back at the carnival." Pa Charlie leaned over and gave Molly-Mae a kiss on her cheek. Molly-Mae turned apple-red, a shocking contrast to her spun-sugar-white hair.

Everyone was up on their feet in an instant, yelping and hugging, handing out congratulations.

"We'd love that!" Tempest said, but I could see through her faux-cheerfulness, of course. She was upset with me.

Well, I was upset with everything and everyone.

I muttered some kind of congratulations to Molly-Mae and Pa Charlie, but I scuffed my feet through the seashell gravel and went off on my own back to the darkened midway.

Mama would be here to share Pa Charlie's wedding day with him.

Aunt Grania would leave by then.

I found myself at Tempest's booth, and sat down there. A few pieces of junk were left on the table: a pair of scissors, three tiny little screws, a magnifying glass, a thin strip of magnet, like Mama and Tempest used sometimes when they were crafting.

I toyed with the bendable magnet in my hands. Tempest had said her newest invention was all about magnets. About the tides. About us. But how, exactly?

I folded the strip of magnet, nearly snapping it in two. Then I remembered something. When Tempest had been preparing for her magnet presentation, she'd shown me how you can snip a magnet in half with a pair of scissors. They become two separate magnets then, creating new poles at each end: south and north, one positive, one negative. Like slicing an earthworm in half. Start with one, end with two.

Tempest had pushed the two new magnets toward each other after she'd cut them apart, and they'd repelled, their like poles pushing against each other. It was a weird sensation, trying to force two magnets toward each other but not being able to do it. That invisible press was powerful and mysterious, like a living thing with an iron will.

It was very much like the feeling when Tempest had reached for my elbow a few minutes ago, right here on the midway.

A thought bubbled up to the surface of my mind, circling there for a second, just out of reach. Then it forced itself to the front of my brain, exploding large and loud.

Magnets.

No.

No. I tried not to even let myself think it, but of course I did. I connected the dots. I saw everything so clearly.

It all made sense then.

Me. Tempest.

Mama. Aunt Grania.

"Never my choice," Mama had said.

"You don't have a clue what you're talking about," Aunt Grania had told me.

Grandma Greenly and her sister, quilting via the postal service.

Separated sisters. The Greenly Curse.

My stomach roiled. This couldn't be true.

I managed to make it to the stand of dogwood bushes past the animal tent before I threw up.

12

The next day I did my morning chores, avoiding everyone and everything that I could, feeling surly. It had been an extra-long night of tossing and turning, of trying to talk myself out of the realization I had faced last night, wishing I had the rhythm of Bones's breathing to help me get to sleep. Instead, I had a little ball of rage shimmying around in my midsection, wanting to scream at both my sister and my aunt, and my mama too, for good measure.

When I had gathered my wits I went to confront Aunt Grania. But I couldn't find her anywhere.

"Fat Sam said she and Molly-Mae went wedding shopping in Brunswick," Digger said when I found him and Tempest sitting at one of the picnic tables outside of the Candy Wagon.

"What are you doing?" I asked Tempest, sounding crabby, exactly how I was feeling.

She had her shoebox of junk sitting on the table, but the only thing she'd taken out was an old, tarnished silver spoon. It sat on the table by itself, its handle adorned with an engraved, cursive G. Tempest had her hands folded in her lap, and she stared at that spoon intently.

"Be quiet," Digger warned. "She told me not to talk."

I stole a piece of Digger's elephant ear—with extra powdered sugar—and I thanked the Lord above for Molly-Mae and her way around the deep fryer. Digger shoved the rest of the elephant ear into his mouth at once and tried to talk around it.

I finished my bite. "Wait until you swallow. Jeez, get some manners."

"What's wrong with your sister?" he asked.

"She must be thinking," I said, rolling my eyes.

"I'm not thinking," Tempest answered. "I mean, I am. I'm always thinking. You're always thinking. It's not like we're ever *not* thinking. But I'm doing something else too."

"It doesn't look like you're doing anything but studying that silly spoon," Digger said, giving me a grin.

Tempest gave her head a swift shake and sighed, like she'd given up on something. "You think thoughts are powerful, Tally?" She looked up at me, all earnest-like.

"Of course thoughts are powerful. They're ideas, and ideas are the first step to getting something done."

"No," Tempest said, shaking her head. "More literal-like. I mean *powerful*. Like, can thoughts affect the environment around you?"

"I don't get what you're talking about."

"It doesn't matter." Tempest sighed, picking up the spoon and dropping it into her cardboard box. Then she pulled out a few different things: several small springs, a broken watch, a spool of wire.

Digger chewed loudly, swallowing even more loudly. "I know what you mean, Tempest. You were fixing to bend that spoon with your mind. Is that what you were doing?"

Tempest smiled. "Yeah, exactly. But I couldn't do it."

I looked from Digger to Tempest. "What?"

"It's a thing," Digger explained. "Bending spoons with mind power. Magicians and such do it. Or attempt to. They just try to bend it right at the neck with nothing but their thought waves." Digger waggled his eyebrows.

"That sounds impossible," I said.

"So does levitating a frog, and I did that with Mr. Umberto."

"But that was science. Bending a spoon with thoughts sounds a little bit like . . . magic." Of course, I had to admit to myself that I knew mind power. Had been on the receiving end of it, even. Tempest had kept me from doling out sweet, sweet justice to Bradley Ballard.

Tempest sat up then, pursed her lips. "I think a lot of science can seem like magic before it's explained properly. Sometimes we don't have the observations, the data, or the right words yet to explain it. Surely, there was a time long ago when people watched a butterfly emerge from a chrysalis and thought of it as magic."

"If I saw you levitate a frog, I'd probably think you were a witch," Digger offered.

"I would think it was magic if you ever seemed to comb your hair in the morning," I told Digger.

"Not magic," he said. "Just the apocalypse." He brought his baseball hat out from his back pocket and put it on his head.

Tempest had a couple of tiny screws held between her lips now, and she worked to unfasten the back of the watch with a miniature Phillips-head screwdriver, but that didn't stop her from talking. "I read something fascinating. Ice crystals, while they're forming, they create beautiful patterns if people think good thoughts around them. And they make nasty, ugly, asymmetrical patterns when people focus their bad attitudes on them."

I gave Digger a look. "Your parents must've really focused their bad thoughts on you when you were forming."

Tempest laughed then, spitting the screws from her lips. And the corners of my lips tipped up, wanting to smile, though I didn't let them. But inside, I enjoyed Tempest's laugh—it was something I'd missed. It was a clear, two-note jingle-bell sound. Such a good sound.

Digger was laughing too. "Oh, Tally Jo, you are gonna get it for that one." He lifted the paper plate that had held his elephant ear and he blew on it. All the extra powdered sugar puffed straight into my face.

I inhaled at just the exact wrong moment and I choked on it, coughing hard. Digger said, "Powdered-sugar lung. You deserve it, Tally." Tempest's eyes crinkled at the corners as she watched me wipe my face. She and Digger laughed some more.

Though part of me wanted to laugh with them, I didn't. I just scowled, hacking up powdered sugar and feeling like a storm cloud.

I got up to leave, and Digger grabbed my hand. "No, you don't."

He offered Tempest his other hand and he pulled her up from the picnic table. "That's it. I'm out of patience for you and your crabapple attitude, Tally. You two are coming with me."

Tempest grumbled under her breath as she stuffed her pockets full of her doodads. Then Digger pulled us along toward the Ferris wheel, calling out to his dad, "Fat Sam, you let us ride up to the tippy-top?"

"Sure thing, son."

It was something Digger loved to do: ride the Ferris wheel up to the top and have Fat Sam stop us there, poised above the carnival lot, feeling like the kings and queens of everything below.

"I don't want to ride to the top today," I grouched.

"Too bad," Digger said. "We are going up there, all three of us, and we are going to stay there until you're over this hissy fit you're having."

The authoritative tone in Digger's voice shocked me into silence. "Humph," was all I could think to say.

Soon, we sat three across in one of the orange bucket seats of the Ferris wheel, paused at the top of the ride. Digger sat in the middle, between Tempest and me, rocking the bucket seat.

"Ladies, we're on top of the world right now," Digger said, giving me his most charming, gap-toothed smile.

I didn't return it. Being up in this bucket high in the sky, two feet from my sister, was making it hard to ignore what was making me crabby in the first place. Because *it* was here, right now. Whatever this thing was between my sister and me. And now I knew for sure that it was not something she was engineering.

It was something worse.

Much worse.

It throbbed between us, like a headache starting in your temples, just barely bad enough to be noticed. Like a sore tooth that your tongue can't help but seek out.

It had snuck up on me, but it was there nearly all the time, a fine pressure against my eardrums. Even if I didn't want to admit it.

I tried to find some way to calm my jangled nerves. But it wasn't possible.

I kept picturing the little white shelf above Tempest's bed at home, emptied of her collection, her most favorite rocks and gems that she'd collected over the years: fool's gold, a pretty pink slice of agate, a corked glass bottle of St. Simons black sand.

No more NASA posters on our walls. No more saving the batteries from every lickety-split thing.

Tempest gone. Erased from my life.

Two magnets, two poles, repelling.

No.

I took some deep breaths.

I leaned my head back on the seat and I took in the landscape around us. The day was still and heavy, in the way that only balmy summer days can be, with the hot June, Georgia sun high in its perch. The cicadas sang off in the distance, the crickets answering call resting now in the daylight hours. The carnival itself was quiet, with Hames sweeping the midway, collecting any of yesterday's litter, and Pa Charlie smoking his pipe near the now-dead embers of last night's fire.

Tempest sat with her liar gauge flat in the palm of her hand as we swayed to Digger's motions. Forward, back. Forward, back. She started asking Digger random questions.

Deep breath in.

Deep breath out.

There was no fight that separated Aunt Grania and Mama. It was much worse than that.

I didn't want to have to tell Tempest.

"Do you know the difference between a real and imaginary number?" Tempest asked Digger.

Digger turned red. "Not at the moment."

Tempest opened the back of the liar gauge to fiddle with its innards. She produced some copper wire from her pocket, winding it around a silver gear. "Have you ever been arrested?"

"No ma'am."

Deep breath in.

From up here, you could even see the ocean off in the distance, its rolling waves, white-capped and powerful, washing up on the black-sanded shores of the St. Simons beach. It was full of strange, striated rocks of all sizes, from boulders to the tiniest grains of sand, made from some kind of rare mineral in shades from gunmetal to silver to midnight black. People came from around the world to see the glittery sands on the beach, to pocket a few of its strange metallic grains.

Deep breath out.

Digger rocked the bucket seat something fierce.

"Hey," I warned.

"Did you eat my peanut-butter cookies I left in the mess tent?" Tempest asked.

"No," Digger said, a telltale blush settling in the apples of his cheeks.

"You're lying, Digger Swanson," Tempest announced. She showed him the gadget in her hand. The needle from the pressure gauge waggled back and forth, and Tempest gave Digger a very superior look. She opened the back again and started prodding the mechanism, using one end of the copper wire.

"Anyone could've told you I was lying about that. I love those peanut-butter cookies." Digger laughed, low and hearty. "How's your other invention going? The one with the tides?"

"I'm stuck," Tempest explained. "But that one, it's going to help Tally and me."

"Is it?" Digger asked. "Then why aren't you working on that right now? Isn't it more urgent?" He gave me a look, all side-eyed and skeptical.

"What do you mean by that?" Tempest asked.

Digger explained, "I can sense it too, sitting right here in between y'all. You're fairly crackling with something. Static electricity on steroids." He rocked the bucket seat again. "I'm not a moron, you know. I saw what happened with those matches the other night."

"The moon is extra close to the earth. It happens every few years. I think it's making it worse," Tempest said.

"The Flower Moon," I said.

"Yeah, it's making everything worse."

"Making what worse?" I asked. I knew, of course. I just wanted to hear her say it.

"This thing between us."

What is between us?

I didn't say it out loud. I just thought it to Tempest, without even realizing I was going to do it. I shot that question from my mind to hers.

What do you think? Tempest sent back to me.

Are we the magnets, Tempest? Pushing against each other?

My mind went silent. The quiet sounds of the carnival cleanup below, the whir of the nearby highway, Pa Charlie's booming laughter—all of it went quiet, like someone had hit the mute button. And all I could hear was Tempest's sharp intake of breath when I asked that question.

Yeah, I think so.

I exhaled a deep breath and tried to steady myself. I didn't want to accept this.

Digger was talking still, oblivious. "Y'all fixing to howl at the full moon with Pork Chop?" Digger chuckled. I elbowed him hard in the ribs. How could he be joking at a time like this?

Tempest kept talking, "I looked up the Flower Moon, after Digger told me what y'all had found, and that's what they call it when the moon is as close as possible to Earth."

We all turned our faces upward and checked for the moon in the sky. It wasn't there, of course, as it was high noon. But it felt like the moon could see us, anyway. It was affecting us, surely. It was just . . . hiding, just out of our reach, playing us like puppets.

"So what happens on your birthday?" Digger asked, now serious, suddenly understanding what was at stake.

"Well, I'm . . ." I trailed off. Had Tempest put this part together yet? The obvious next step. Our inevitable conclusion?

Something told me she hadn't. She seemed too calm. If she knew, she'd be freaking out, just like I was inside.

She hadn't yet applied our mess to Aunt Grania and Mama, to their separation. Was I going to have to tell her? My stomach turned at the thought, and I wondered if I might barf again, over the side of the Ferris wheel.

This all seemed impossible. Too impossible to be true.

Tempest had pulled out a bunch of things from her pocket now: a spool of copper wire, three miniscule watch batteries, a tiny set of scissors. "My invention is just stalled right now. I'm not certain of my next step. I have to think on it, the repolarizing," Tempest mumbled, practically talking to herself.

But I needed to know. "So, how will your invention help us?"

Tempest didn't answer me. Maybe she hadn't even heard me. I sighed loudly, but still she didn't look up.

Digger stole a length of copper wire from Tempest's stash.

After a long time, she responded. "I don't know yet. So don't ask me any more questions." She blinked hard once, and then again.

I turned and watched Digger's hands as they began fashioning that length of copper wire into something—twisting it and turning it, bending it to his will.

The wind picked up a little and rocked our Ferris wheel bucket. I laid my head back on the headrest and I closed my eyes. Right in my chest, I felt the pressure of Tempest being so near me.

I took out my inhaler and breathed in twice from it.

Digger was right. It was getting worse. Urgent.

What in the world were we going to do?

Digger had coiled his wire into little springy pieces, and soon it started to take on a shape.

"What is that going to be?" I asked. "A butterfly?"

"A dragonfly," he answered. He motioned to Tempest for another piece, which she produced from the seemingly endless supply in her pockets. Digger bent a longer piece of wire into the second wing, and then I could see what he was trying for. It was really something. He handed it over to me. "For you."

"Thanks." It was light in my hand, bent in such a way that it looked like it was about to take off at any moment.

Digger leaned his head toward me. "Sorry I made werewolf jokes about whatever's going on with you two. I know—"

"It's all right. We just don't know why or what we can do to—"

"What if you don't get this invention done by the time your birthday rolls around?" Digger asked.

My stomach did a backflip, and I looked at Tempest. She said, "Tally and I will have to spend our birthday apart, make sure we're not too close. 'Cause this seems to be gaining steam, doesn't it? We're fairly explosive now, so by then, who knows? Then once the moon passes . . . everything will go back to normal, at least for a while. Until the next moon. Because everything with the moon is a cycle."

This was why Tempest thought we were going to be okay. She didn't realize that after the Flower Moon, it didn't cycle back.

I wished she was right. I did.

But . . . if she was, then Mama and her sister wouldn't have to live half a world apart.

Tempest must've seen it on my face.

The resignation. The impossible sadness of it all.

Tempest stopped speaking, and I watched the color fade from her cheeks. She was finally putting it together, connecting the dots between us and the moon, between Mama and Aunt Grania and their forced separation.

The Flower Moon was not part of a cycle. No. It was the spark, the igniter, blowing this thing between us wide open. Nothing was going to cycle back afterward.

We could look at Mama and Aunt Grania to see that. Or our grandmother and her twin.

Suddenly, Tempest gasped. "No."

"Tempest, I—"

"You already know? When'd you figure it out?"

"Only last night."

"What'd you figure out?" Digger asked.

I lifted my eyes to Digger's. "Don't make me say it."

"Our Mama. And Aunt Grania," Tempest croaked.

Digger's face went serious. "They don't choose to stay apart?"

"No," I answered. "They don't."

"They have to stay apart? They're . . . what? Combustible?" The panic in Digger's eyes was freaking me out. "Tally?" Digger asked, and he grabbed my hand. "Tally, you're shaking."

"We only have six more days," Tempest whispered. She was calmer about this than I thought she'd be. "Six days until the moon comes up on our birthday."

I felt despair, utter despair and anger, but Tempest nodded to herself and then kept winding a piece of copper wire around a wooden spool. I wanted her to react. So I could know she fully understood.

I kept picturing my room without Tempest's stuff in it.

And worse, I thought of Tempest out in this big, mean world without me. Walking strange halls at a strange school, her blinking gone out of control, wearing her hair in those golly-gee pigtails. Who would protect her? Who would be there to defend her from the Bradley Ballards of this world?

Suddenly, I couldn't get a big enough breath. My ribs ached. My throat pinched. I took a deep pull of my inhaler, then another one. Digger whistled through the gap in his teeth for Fat Sam to let us down.

I couldn't say I'd be sorry to get away from my sister right then. Fat Sam threw the lever, and the wheel began to move, slow but sure, our car traveling back toward the ground.

"Listen, Tempest, there's got to be something we can do. I'm going to talk to Pa and Grania, find out what Mama and Grania tried at least, and then . . . I don't know . . . I'll find a way to protect you from this, and—"

"Tally, you're exhausting me." Tempest eyed the stuff in her palms. "I'm trying to make something here. Don't you have any faith in me?"

I eyed her bits and bobs, her spool of copper wire. "It's just . . . this thing is bigger than some kind of jerry-rigged doo-hickey, and—"

"Oh, right," she said, shoving all her stuff into her pockets. The Ferris wheel came to a stop and Fat Sam steadied our bucket, lifted the lap bar. "I could never fix anything big, could never do anything important. That job is only for Tally Jo Trimble, not geeky old Tempest and her box of bolts," she said, her words clipped and sharp. "Tally, why can't you even believe in me just a little bit?"

And with that, Tempest took off in a huff.

I hurried right out of the bucket seat too, needing to get away from Tempest, needing to get a better breath into my lungs.

"What's the hurry?" Fat Sam called after me, but I ignored him as I strode away. I heard Tempest calling back to Digger to ask if we had found any scrap metal in the catch-all.

"Probably," he answered her.

But I kept on moving toward the pod. On my own. All alone.

I figured I'd better get used to it.

13

Once the carnival started up that evening and I had calmed myself down enough to be fit for human company, I found Digger in the animal tent. "Where's Aunt Grania?" I asked him. "Nobody's seen her, and I want to ask her what they tried, if anything, and—"

"Tally, wait," Digger said. Then I saw what was in his arms, and I forgot all about Aunt Grania and Mama. Digger gently placed a listless Pork Chop into the crook of my arm. "He's not feeling well."

"I see that."

"He was curled up in a far corner of the animal tent, away from the other pups. I reckon his stomach's aching. Left a pile of vomit over in the corner. I'm going to put up the closed sign."

I stroked the crown of Pork Chop's head. "It's okay, little guy." I found a spot on the hay bale in the corner, and I sat with him in my lap, careful not to jostle him. When Digger reappeared, I said, "He feels warm. Did he seem warm to you?"

"I'm not good at this stuff, Tally. I didn't notice."

Pork Chop looked skinny as a Popsicle stick. I could even see a hint of his ribs. I gingerly picked him up and tried to palpate his abdomen, like I'd seen Dr. Fran do a thousand times to the dogs.

Pork Chop did not like that. He turned and nipped at my hand, then slithered out of my grip and wouldn't let me back near him. Digger and I got him cornered behind the water bowl, and Pork Chop actually bared his teeth at me.

I gave Digger some orders, and when he returned, I sat on the ground near Pork Chop and was able to coax him out with a Tupperware bowl full of oatmeal mixed with diced-up ham.

This had him crawling over me like I was his new best friend. He licked the Tupperware clean, and I felt all kinds of proud of myself because I'd had Digger hide some tummy-soothing jasmine rice in there—a trick I'd learned from Dr. Fran. "You must've eaten something that didn't agree with you," I told Pork Chop, scratching at his ears for him.

What a relief it was when Pork Chop scuttled into my lap, sniffed at my T-shirt and chin, and curled himself into a ball to sleep.

"Thank goodness," Digger said, going off to do our chores.

Molly-Mae appeared soon after, carrying a plastic-wrapped plate full of her famous fried chicken.

"Just wanted to check up on the poor pup," she said, "and bring you something to eat."

"Thanks. I think he's on the mend," I said.

Molly-Mae hesitated. "You look like you could use some company," she said, placing the paper plate on her lap as she sat down on a hay bale across from me.

"Just worrying over Pork Chop."

Molly-Mae tilted her head and smiled. "Aside from the dark hair, you look so much like your mother, Tally. It's really striking."

"Do I?"

"You'll be a great beauty one day."

"Who cares about that?" I grumbled, eyeing the plate of fried chicken. Pork Chop gave a little whimper from his position in my lap, and I tried to sit still so as to not jostle him. I would eat later.

Molly-Mae patted at her hairdo in her nervous way. "Tally, I reckon I was just trying to give you a chance to talk to me . . . You seem so out of sorts lately."

Ugh. I'd hurt Molly-Mae's feelings. Why was everyone so sensitive? I didn't have time for that.

Unless . . .

"Actually, I was wanting to talk to you," I told Molly-Mae. Her eyes brightened, and I went on. "You were on our list of interrogations that we wanted to get done." I smiled to myself. The list I made with Digger. It seemed so long ago already—and now so unimportant. We knew too much now, and yet not nearly enough.

"Your pa said you were asking about your mother and Grania."

"Yep, I was."

"They have a thorny history. One I'm not exactly supposed to be talking about with you."

"I'm kind of tired of that excuse," I said, sighing.

She didn't say a thing, which was very uncharacteristic for Molly-Mae. I took advantage.

"Listen, Molly-Mae, let me level with you. We know that Mama and Aunt Grania didn't choose to be separated." Her eyebrows shot up at that, but she didn't say a word, so I continued. "What I need to know is what they tried. In order to stay together. I mean, I—" I choked up here for just a second, thinking about my sister.

"Tally, this is hard for your pa to talk about, I reckon." Molly-Mae leaned over and patted my leg in a very grandmotherly gesture. "When Grania decided to leave, it was—"

"Whoa, wait. She *did* decide to leave?"

"Well, yes, Grania left. Your mama wanted more time to try out a bunch of things, but . . ."

I sat up straighter, just barely stopping myself from startling Pork Chop. "So I was right! Aunt Grania *did* bail on Mama. Completely!" Just like I'd thought. Sure, this whole thing was inevitable. But Aunt Grania had left Mama before they could even try to fix it.

Never my choice.

Molly-Mae was still talking. "I don't know if I would say she *bailed*, Tally. Oh, Tally, I so want to be able to comfort you. I do. But I don't know what to say about this here conundrum between your mama and Grania. Not sure it's my place to—"

"Molly-Mae, do you have any of Mama's old silhouette garlands?"

"I don't think so, Tally."

I wanted to find more notes, more information. But I knew there was really only one way to get it. I had to talk to Aunt Grania.

Even if my blood boiled at the thought of her.

Poor Pork Chop jerked in my lap then, a full-body cringe, bringing himself to a sitting position. Then he retched once, twice, finally throwing up some kind of greenish substance in the hay next to us.

"Ooh, boy," Molly-Mae said. "I was hoping he was over the worst of it."

I stroked Pork Chop from head to tail, comforting him, dipping my hand into the water dish and offering him my fingers to lick. He did, which I thought was a good sign. "You can go, Molly-Mae. I'll take care of him. Digger'll be back right quick."

She pressed a hand all tender-like to the crown of my head. Then she left.

Soon, poor Pork Chop wouldn't be comforted. He left my lap, and all he would do was hide behind his water dish and whimper. He wouldn't let me near him again, and every few minutes, he would brace himself, stiff and stilted, holding real still, like he was fighting against some unknown pain. He couldn't even be distracted from his suffering with a bite of Molly-Mae's chicken.

Pork Chop's brothers and sister tried to nose their way around him a few times, tried to hop and jump, nip and snarl at him, even howl toward the evening moon—anything to get him to chase, to play.

They whimpered too, when Pork Chop wouldn't join in. They were worried about their sibling.

Didn't I know how that felt?

The noises of the carnival went on outside the tent: all the muted voices and jingling-jangling carnival bells, but what I was really listening to was Pork Chop's labored breathing. Every difficult inhale, every weak exhale, slow and uneven, as he lay listless behind his water bowl.

I reached out, trying to pet the poor pup between the ears or coax him from his hiding spot, but he growled and sank his teeth into my fingers, drawing a bit of blood from my thumb. So instead I watched him stand up on shaky legs and circle and circle his area behind the water dish, sniffing here and there at a piece of hay, and whimpering.

But then, as he crossed next to the hay bale, he tottered on his legs, and then they gave out from under him. He fell, suddenly too weak to hold himself up or to fight me holding him. He let me take him into my lap, and I admitted to myself that I was very, very scared.

Pork Chop was hot as the Georgia asphalt in July.

"Digger!" I called, trying not to let the terror show in my voice, trying not to scream too loud and scare the wolf pup.

Digger came running. "Get your dad," I told him.

When Fat Sam came in, he took one look at the poor little pup in my lap and asked, "Tally, is he breathing still?"

"Yes. But he's burning up." Pork Chop's eyes were sunken, glazed over.

After a quick examination, Fat Sam sighed heavy and deep. "There's nothing to be done, that I can tell. We can go to the vet in the morning, but I think all we can do now, Tally Jo . . . I mean, he was the runt. Maybe he wasn't healthy to begin with and—"

"Don't say it," I said. "I don't want to hear it."

"We can make him comfortable. That's all."

"Leave us alone," I barked at Fat Sam.

"I'll stay with you—" Digger started.

"No." I blinked back the tears.

"Tally," Digger said. "I can—"

"No, please. Just go."

I knew they were looking at each other, deciding what to do, but they did end up leaving me with Pork Chop. His breath was starting to slow, turn more shallow, his eyes glassy and heavy-lidded.

His tense muscles seemed to relax a bit though. I hoped he could get some sleep. Maybe that would be enough to help him fight off whatever this was. I stroked the curve of his backbone, and I sang to him, soft, happy songs. I didn't give up.

I racked my brain trying to think what Dr. Fran might tell me to do, what idea I might have missed. This time when I dribbled some water from my fingertips onto his muzzle, he didn't stir.

I didn't realize I was falling asleep, but I woke to the worried whinnying of Antique as he looked on from his stall.

"It'll be all right," I told Antique. "It'll be all right." I wished I believed it.

The pup, his little ribs barely rose and fell now. It wasn't going to be long.

I stilled my own breathing, slowed it to match his. I let myself fall into that pup's groove. "What is wrong, little one?"

I couldn't bear if he died, not today. Not now. Not when so much else was going on around us.

Selfishly, I told him, *It's not a good time. I need you.*

And then I thought of what Tempest had told me:

You've got something too.

And the pup squirmed under my chin, his scruff soft and fine next to the sensitive skin of my neck, and I felt something. A bristly warmth, coming from the pup himself, quivering off him.

Was it his hurt?

It had an odd, uncomfortable undercurrent that settled at the base of my skull and ached. Something in me wanted to run out of the animal tent, get Digger to watch Pork Chop, and never look back. But I knew I couldn't do that. No.

I wasn't going to *bail*.

Instead, I opened myself up to Pork Chop. I listened, with all of my power, my hopes, and my strength. I listened with my heart, with all that I had in me.

Whatever was coming from him, it radiated toward me with more force now. From his heart to mine. He was speaking.

I just had to know how to listen.

And instantly I knew what had happened.

I saw it, exactly how it had played out. It had been hidden in the straw on the ground, no bigger than a quarter. But too big, too sharp, rusty at one end.

Pork Chop had swallowed a roofing nail. It was caught in his insides, past his belly, but not far enough past, and if left there, it would be the end of him.

I sat up straight, gently trying to rearrange Pork Chop in my arms as I stood. I turned toward the door of the tent, the quiet darkness of the night around me, the straw crunching under my feet, and I stopped short when I saw that there, curled up near the door, was Digger Swanson himself.

"Digger," I said, my voice crackling with sleep, with fear. "We need to get your daddy and call an all-night vet. I know what's wrong."

14

I woke to the noise of someone turning the handle on the pod's flimsy aluminum door. I jumped right out of the bed, confused and bleary-eyed, and grabbed the baseball bat that I always kept propped in the corner. I kicked the door wide open and darn near clocked Digger Swanson in his mouth with the Louisville Slugger.

"Digger, you dumb cluck!" I hissed at him, lowering the bat. "You want to get yourself killed?"

"He's fine. He made it," Digger said, his face split into a grin. "He made it through surgery like a champ."

I caught up to what he was saying. "Pork Chop?"

"The vet says he's going to be fine. You saved him, Tally Jo."

I let out a little surprised laugh, tears prickling at my eyes. I looked beyond Digger standing outside my trailer door, and took in the lavender light growing near the horizon. It wasn't even dawn yet. Fat Sam had made me come home from the vet's office once we'd dropped Pork Chop off, near midnight. "You gotta get some sleep, Tally Jo, or your grandpa will hide me," he'd said.

I grabbed Digger in a hug, and he pulled me out of the trailer, swung me around. "Pork Chop's okay! Can we go see him?"

Digger set me down. "Keep your voice down, Tally. Now go get changed. You have to come with me out to Fort Frederica. We'll take a couple of the old bikes Fat Sam's fixed up."

"Can't we go see Pork Chop?"

Digger shook his head. "Not until afternoon. Doctor's orders."

"So you want to go to the graveyard?" I rolled my eyes at Digger.

He nodded. "Of course."

"What is it with you and that place?"

"Come on. We just cheated death for that little wolf pup. We need to celebrate. Or are you too chicken?" He narrowed his eyes at me, and I knew I would go.

"All right. Wait here," I said. "Let me throw some clothes on."

"I knew you'd say yes," Digger said. "I'm irresistible."

"Is that right?"

"The ladies love the gap in my teeth," he said, whistling through it while he shut the door to the trailer behind him.

I eyed Tempest, still sleeping despite all the commotion, and I thought about waking her to come along. But then I didn't do it. Not because I didn't want her there; it wasn't that. I just didn't want to face . . . *us* right now. I felt strangely optimistic. I didn't want reality to squash it just yet.

I put my hair into a ponytail, pulled on my shorts and T-shirt, and searched under my bed for my gym shoes.

I was officially avoiding my sister. And everything we needed to face.

But Pork Chop was okay; that little wisp of an animal who weighed no more than a particularly large melon had stared into the great abyss and had come back. He'd beaten it. I'd helped him beat it, some magical, weirdo way, and that wasn't nothing.

I shoved my feet into my beat-up sneakers, and I thought of Pork Chop's little ears, the soft, silky fluff just around the inside edge. My throat tightened, and I felt a thrill of shaky, uncertain hope toward . . . everything. If I didn't look right into the bare reality of what Tempest and I had going on between us . . . if I looked at it only out of the corner of my eye, then I could even feel a little hopeful about it too. I wasn't helpless.

I felt powerful.

Fort Frederica was an old army deal, with lots of bricks lying around that you were supposed to care about, showing you where houses used to be way back even before America was America. It was kind of interesting, with the ruins of a whole little town, an old fortress, and a hand-mortared stone wall, plus a couple of real ancient cannons. But the best thing to see was the graveyard. It sat down in a shaded gulley surrounded by stands of white birches that held wisps of Spanish moss and kudzu. The tombstones were barely more than flat rocks, with hand-carved names and dates in them. Death seemed to be all around this place, and the gravestones told the stories. Children and soldiers, whole families, buried with these sad and patriotic sayings.

The gulley was unexpectedly chilly as Digger and I roamed around the cemetery itself, reading the epitaphs, thinking our own thoughts. Then Digger tripped over something and fell rear end over elbow right into my path.

"What are you doing?" I said, giving him a little kick in his backside.

"Thought I was gonna die for a second," he said, laughing. "Almost hit my head on that gravestone."

"Your hard head wouldn't have minded," I told him. But then I caught some movement out of the corner of my eye. "Something's coming," I said, pulling Digger down to a kneeling position like me. I pointed over toward the stand of birches across the cemetery.

"Look, there," I whispered.

The air shimmered and moved in a surprising way. It was there, then gone, just a wavy trick of the light, radiating the way campfire flames or hot sun on the concrete like to play with your vision. Goose bumps raised on my arms and the back of my neck.

"What the heck is that?" Digger asked.

"Just the fog," I answered, both relieved and disappointed. "Early morning fog." I saw it coming, just a hint of it at first, appearing out of nowhere, hovering above the ground. Then the birch branches swayed, and sure as rhubarb pie, a fine mist rolled quietly over the ground like a blanket.

Digger began walking over there and I followed. The fog thickened, making it difficult to see below our ankles.

"You believe in ghosts and stuff, Tally?" Digger asked, using the heel of his hand to rub the dirt off a cupid's face on one of the fancier carved headstones.

"I don't know. Probably not."

"Why not?"

"Most stuff usually has a good explanation. Science. Like how this was just fog."

"What about what's going on with you and your sister?" Digger said.

"What's that got to do with anything?"

"Sometimes impossible things are true things."

I thought again of what Tempest had called magic: science we don't have the words for yet. I didn't feel like having this conversation with Digger though, so I just said, "You know what I think is truly impossible? Believing a word you have to say."

Digger laughed, loud and clear. It made me smile. And then he plopped down and sat cross-legged on the ground, swirling his hand through the fog. I settled down next to him and did the same.

"People are starting to notice," Digger said. "Not just me."

"Yeah." I knew he meant what was between Tempest and me. Yesterday, I'd seen how Arnie Schutes looked at the two of us out near the game alley, when something had erupted between us hard and strong, a burst of pressure that nearly sent me backwards onto my butt.

"You gotta fight it, Tally Jo. Dig in."

"I know, Digger. I do." I swallowed around something then. "But how exactly am I supposed to fight it?"

"It's like you've got something, Tally. Just like Tempest told you."

This seemed unbelievable, at least when I heard the words said out loud. I shook my head, doubting my optimism from earlier. "I don't have anything, Digger. Tempest's the one. She's the magic."

"I don't know if that's true. You saved Pork Chop."

I lifted my hand through the fog, tried to catch it in between my fingertips. It was elusive, like so many things.

"I did save Pork Chop." I smiled. We sat there for a while, thinking our own thoughts, listening to the crickets.

"Fog's weird," I said. "There, but not there."

"Like chiffon."

"What's that?"

"It's a fabric. I went to the seventh-grade dance with this girl named Erika, and she wore a dress made out of chiffon. Turquoise. The fog reminds me of it."

I stiffened at this. Digger at a dance? With a girl? "There's a kid at school who likes me," I blurted out.

"Yeah?" Digger said, and I tried not to be pleased at how Digger seemed a little ruffled, scratching at his neck, looking everywhere but at me. "What's his name?"

"Seth. Seth Bowers. Follows me around, always asking me to go to Reed's and get ice cream after school."

"Is he a dork?"

"No, he's all right."

Digger nodded, and I cleared my throat, wondering what in the world had made me bring up Seth Bowers. Digger changed the subject, thank the high heavens.

"You don't like your aunt too much, huh?"

"I don't know." I couldn't quit thinking about that stupid turquoise dress. Chiffon. That was a weird word.

"You're blaming your aunt for . . . whatever."

"I'm not blaming her. I just think maybe she could be more honest with us, and maybe they gave up too soon and—"

"You should give her a chance, Tally. I see the way you look at her like she peed in your Kool-Aid."

That got a laugh out of me.

Then Digger got all serious on me. "Maybe she's just doing what she thinks is best, and this whole wacky situation isn't anyone's—"

Suddenly, I didn't like how he was telling me what to do, as if I wasn't worried enough about this. As if I wasn't taking seriously what was going on between Tempest and me, what had been handed down to us from my mother and Aunt Grania. "Digger, maybe you don't know a lick of what you're talking about."

"Maybe I do. With my parents' divorce, I guess . . . things happen. Sometimes there are sides, blame to be put on people. But sometimes, I don't know. Bad things just happen. And then you're just left with *what is* . . . and you have to find something inside your own self to set things right."

I remembered Digger's mother's fiery red hair, the way she burned in the summer sun. She always loved me, sneaking me my favorite potato chips from the Candy Wagon and telling me I was a good friend to Digger.

I watched Digger watching me, and I saw a change in his face then, like something had cracked wide open and I was getting to see the real Digger, the inside of him.

And I felt rotten and guilty for not comforting him one lick over his parents' divorce this whole time. I was so wrapped up in my own business lately, wasn't I?

It was on the tip of my tongue to apologize to Digger, for being so prickly, for never listening . . . I don't know, for just in general being a bad friend who never really gave him the time of day. But I couldn't do it. The words just sort of dried up on my tongue.

I didn't know why I found it so hard to be nice and say sorry to Digger, but I did. So instead of saying something he needed to hear, instead of being the friend I knew I should be, I swatted a mosquito off his cheek, darn near slapping him in the face.

"You're welcome," I said, and I took off back toward the carnival, fighting tears all the way.

15

When I returned from the graveyard I snuggled back into bed, determined to sleep, even though it was late in the morning. But the chirping birds outside our pod window had other ideas. Soon, I heard Tempest come in, along with the *clink-clank* of her box of junk.

I pulled the bedspread over my head and tried to ignore her. I felt her there though, in my molars and in the pressure behind my eyes. I hated this thing between us, hated it worse than a million Bradley Ballards.

"Did you have fun with Digger this morning?" she said, an edge in her voice.

"I guess," I mumbled, sticking my head out from under the blanket. "What are you up to?"

"Clock's ticking." She paused. "You didn't ask me to come with you."

"I didn't want to wake you."

"Oh, right."

"What's that supposed to mean?"

"Don't make excuses for not wanting me around."

"Tempest." Suddenly, I was just so exhausted. So much had happened. I was tired from the night with Pork Chop, but I also realized that I was tired from constantly fighting this growing push between Tempest and me. When we were around each other, it was work.

Actual, physical work.

I felt suddenly wistful for last summer. I had a memory, just a simple one, nothing special: just Tempest, Digger, and me hanging out at the St. Simons Pier, eating coconut shrimp from Daisy's Diner, a double order wrapped up in a grease-stained brown paper bag. We'd leaned over the rail of the pier, looking down at the ocean, laughing hard about something stupid that Digger had said.

I wanted that back. I threw the quilt over my head.

"Tally, you listening to me?" Tempest asked.

"Yeah," I answered, my voice breaking. And right then, I was one second from tears. I missed my sister something fierce. I hid my face under my bedcovers and blinked hard.

Tempest continued, "I'm trying to finagle some kind of invention to . . . I don't even know yet. It's just . . . I really . . . I don't want us to have to get separated, Tally. Do you?"

What a ridiculous question that was. I tried to answer, but I couldn't seem to form the words around the lump in my throat.

Tempest took my silence to mean something else. Her voice was a whisper. "Are you happier if you have an excuse to just leave me out of things? Is that why you haven't even tried to fix this between us? You'd finally be rid of me. You could go live your life alone, happier than all get out. Like Aunt Grania."

"You're not making sense," I croaked. How could she think that? *She* was the one like Aunt Grania, going off and leaving me.

I threw the quilt off of myself, sat up, and looked at Tempest. It struck me, the way she held her shoulder, her defensive posture, the way she blinked hard.

"You hate my pigtails," she said.

"Tempest . . ." My throat pinched with something akin to guilt.

"I embarrass you at school because I'm . . . odd."

"None of that is true," I told her, but I couldn't meet her eyes.

"Feels true."

"Don't say that. This is *killing* me, Tempest. I just wish that we could go back to how—"

"Don't," Tempest said, her lips pursing in anger. "Don't wish us back to how we used to be."

"Why?" I said, my tears turning to anger now.

Tempest pushed her box of junk over, emptying the contents on her bed with a loud clanging crash. "Things are never going to go back to how they used to be, Tally Jo. Get used to it. It's called growing up!"

"No, I won't get used to it." I stood up, my arms folded across my chest, bracing for an argument. "Don't you miss us?"

She turned, her hands on her hips. "Of course I do. But things change. People change. Everything changes. The universe is in flux. Energy reinventing itself constantly."

"Great time for a science lecture."

"Oh, right. Sorry! You don't want me, your stupid, nerdy sister, to embarrass you with my geeky habits."

"Tempest, come on. You're the one who's so busy with this techno-garbage. Admit it, you have no time for us any—"

"You know what, Tally? Just stop. I don't follow you around anymore and do everything you say exactly how you say it. So, what? You're unhappy? Well, guess what, Tally? I couldn't live my life just being your sidekick for all eternity just because it pleased you. Or because I was scared of everything and everyone. I had to get brave and become *me*. I had to reach deep inside myself and find out who I wanted to be. And I did that. For God's sake, it was hard, and it was scary, but I became me. And then I wasn't just your shadow. But guess what? I lost you!" She paused, and I could see she was shaking now, with fury or hurt. "I am *me* now, Tally." She straightened her shoulders, composing herself. Then she said, in a whisper, "But I could still use a friend."

"Tempest, I—"

"But you never really wanted me to be one, did you?" Her eyes flashed at me. "Not unless you could tell me exactly what to do, not unless I was nothing but your faithful assistant. You just want to pick and choose exactly how we change, and you don't get to do that. Not everything about me is your decision. See, you went and grew up and away from me too, you know? Cooler, funnier, student council president, your head bent close to Digger Swanson over the campfire with no room for me to join in, you and Marisol going off with Elena to the mall, you and Seth Bowers going to Reed's. See, stuff like that, if it's your idea, it doesn't count. To you, I'm the only one changing."

Something pushed me back on my heels, and it wasn't the physical push that was always there between my sister and me now. No, it was more than that. It was the power of those words.

There was some truth there.

And I had to sit down onto the bed just to keep from losing my balance. Because what Tempest said was bowling me over.

I sat there, dumbfounded. Was that all true? I didn't say anything; I was too busy trying to process her words.

Tempest laughed, this sad, lonely sound. "Forget it. Just go back to blaming me. Seems like the only thing you're really putting all your energy into."

"Tempest, I—" I stood up, wanting to grab her arm, keep her here. But I didn't.

"Right. I'm leaving." Tempest threw a few things back in her cardboard box, but then she stopped. Her body went rigid, and she balled her fists at her sides. She screamed—a tiny, raspy noise of frustration. It hurt me to hear it.

Then she spun around and she stuck her chin out at a defiant angle, shoving her feet into her flip-flops. "Maybe if I was one of your animals, maybe then you might take a minute to consider what it feels like to be me."

My voice came out all strangled. "Tempest, I just want—"

"Stop!" Tempest's shoulders fell, her fury seeming to disappear in an instant. She just looked tired and sad. "Listen. If you'd quit trying so hard to hold on to what we were, you might see what we—each of us, alone and together—can become."

I didn't answer.

She left me standing in the little space between our beds, in our pod, confused, so very sad, and somehow a little guilty.

I scowled at myself and grabbed my inhaler. I gave myself a puff. Two. Still, I couldn't get ahead of it.

I sat on the bed, laid back on my pillow, trying to relax my diaphragm like the doc had told me, and I took two more puffs.

I wondered if guilt could make your lungs tighten up. It sure as shampoo felt like it.

I lay on my bed for a while just feeling sorry for myself, until I spied the red-framed silhouette garland on the wall. Those two little cut-out girls were bent toward each other, frozen together for all eternity, happily so.

I didn't have time for wallowing. I had to *do* something.

It was time for Aunt Grania to come clean, and I intended to make her. But I'd have to be smart, use enough finesse so I didn't get her too worried about Tempest and me. She couldn't go calling Mama. Not yet.

So I went hunting for my aunt. I looked in her trailer and the animal tent, and I was halfway out to the old airplane hangar where Fat Sam said she'd gone to do yoga when I saw her leaning against the Candy Wagon, eating a slice of watermelon like she didn't have a care in the world.

I marched right up to her. "Tell me about what keeps you and Mama apart."

She started to deny it, but I just shook my head. "No. The truth. No more half-truths and avoidance, Aunt Grania. I know there's something between you and Mama, because there's something between Tempest and me." The words were jarring, said out loud like that, and I had to fight for breath around them. "I need to know everything you know, and everything you've tried. Right now."

Sometime during my speech, she'd dropped her watermelon rind right onto the midway and didn't even seem to have noticed. Her mouth was hanging open. She brought one startled hand to her cheek, her bracelets jangling as they dropped to her elbow. "It's already starting?" She took a step closer to me, fear in her eyes. "What's happened?"

"I think you know. There's something pushing us apart. A force. I'm sure you're familiar with it."

She turned so pale then, and she started to ask something, but I held up my hand. "I'll answer all your questions, but first, please, *please*, can you just give me some answers? What happened with you and Mama? Did you try any way to fight it? I need to know."

I watched Aunt Grania process it all, and she took an agonizingly long time before she said, "You're only just turning thirteen, right?"

I nodded. "In a couple days."

"It can't be coming to a head yet. Not until you're eighteen. That's when it happened with us, and with our mother and her twin."

"Maybe we're just . . . getting some early warnings." I wanted to believe that. I considered it, letting the idea roll around in my noggin for a moment. Could we possibly have a few years still?

I tried to believe it. But it felt foolish to doubt the strength of what was growing between Tempest and me. It lived deep beneath my ribs, constant now and growing. I could feel it even with Tempest halfway across the carnival lot. That throb of pressure, always there, told me it was in charge. And that we did not have years at all.

We had days.

But I didn't tell that to Aunt Grania. No, I kept it to myself. And let me tell you, that felt reckless. Reckless, but necessary—I needed every last second I could get with my sister.

"How long did it take? When did you first notice it?" I asked.

"It started gradually, took about a year. How long has it been for—"

"Not long. Weeks."

"Your mom and I, we didn't tell anyone at first. In fact, I made your mother promise she wouldn't." Aunt Grania cringed at her own words, and I thought of the note on the back of the silhouette garland, their shared secrets. "It was a mistake," she finished, quirking an eyebrow at me, as if she was prompting me to confess.

I held my tongue.

Aunt Grania shot me a grave look. "Does your mother know it's started?"

"No."

"Go find your sister, Tally Jo. Then we'll have a talk. But Tally?"

I had already turned to leave. I looked back at Aunt Grania. "What?"

"I don't have a lot of good things to say. I don't want to give you hope. This—whatever this is—it's bigger than us. Bigger than you." And Aunt Grania's face crumpled, as if she was fighting tears. It was just a second before she composed herself again. But I'd seen it. In that flash, I'd seen her pain.

That look—her defeatedness—it made me mad all of a sudden. I turned back without so much as a nod. And inside I thought one word.

Coward.

I knew it was uncharitable. I didn't care.

Aunt Grania had just given up. She had *left* Mama. I knew it for sure now.

And I knew another thing.

Maybe she couldn't figure out how to fight this thing. But I could.

I would.

I was Tally Jo Trimble. Fearless, like my granny.

I was not *scared*.

I mean, I was. But not too scared to try. I was powerful. And I was not just going to accept that I had to live a life without my sister in it.

I needed to go get Tempest.

And there was no time to waste. I looked up into the early morning sky, the orange sun already blazing hot, though hazy behind a film of clouds. I squinted as I looked in the opposite direction, toward the west—and just like I knew it would be, it was there. Just a shadow of itself, white and washed-out like a cloud, translucent like silk, but nearly full and round.

A reminder. A ticking clock.

An hourglass nearly full of sand.

The moon. Fading from sight, surely. But always there. Throbbing like a pulse.

Counting down.

16

I found Fat Sam behind the animal tent, crouched down and working on one of his refurbished 1950s bicycles, sparkling red with a jaunty silver stripe.

"Can I borrow one of your bikes again, Fat Sam? I need to get to the beach."

"Of course."

But then I had a better idea. "Actually, can I take Antique?"

Fat Sam looked up from polishing the fenders. "Kiddo, no, that's not safe."

"Just a short, little, tiny ride?"

"Tally Jo—"

"It's early. Nobody's quite up and about on the island. I just want to take him for a trot on the beach. Real slow-like and safe. I'll take the old trail through the meadow, down by the Coast Guard, and use the public beach access on Dovetail Road. I won't go near streets or people or the pier." I crossed my fingers behind my back. This was an emergency, after all.

Fat Sam wiped the sweat from his brow with a gingham handkerchief. "I suppose I do owe you, after what you did for that little pup."

"You do. Absolutely. You owe me big time." I smiled and bounced from one foot to the other.

"Okay, but don't make me regret this, Tally Jo. Be back in one hour," he called after me. But I was already halfway into the animal tent, where I grabbed Antique's saddle off its peg and whistled for my horse.

I knew where I had to go. It was like always. Hide-and-go-seek.

Tempest was upset with me; I knew that. She wanted to think, somewhere quiet. The beach was a good spot for that.

But it wasn't really logic that led me to Tempest.

I just had a built-in Tempest compass. I always had.

And Digger Swanson was right. I had to dig in and try. I had to show Tempest that I was not okay with the idea of us being separated.

I was the girl sheltering her sister in Mama's silhouette garland. The protector.

I was the leader, the twin in charge. And did I ever feel like it, trotting toward the shore on my glorious horse.

The tide was coming in, the whitecaps breaking over the black sandy beach, then retreating again, leaving the strange, black-and-silver grains glinting in the morning sun.

Antique shook his head, whinnying with sheer joy. He loved the beach. I stroked his neck and laid my head against his silky mane as he trotted along the shoreline, his hooves kicking up the sand and surf.

I spied Tempest on the stretch of beach just past the ancient lighthouse. The pier wasn't far off in the background, white picket railings against a now-darkening sky. Storm clouds were rolling in fast.

Tempest strolled away from Antique and me, her face tilted toward the ocean as she watched the waves.

Her gait was unhurried, with no destination. I watched as she bent to pick up a shell or a rock or some such oddity. She studied it closely, then pocketed it in her cargo shorts. Her posture though, it looked so defeated. Lonely.

It hurt me.

I protected my sister. It's what I did.

I had to fix this.

I hopped off Antique, led him up to the boardwalk near the lighthouse, and tied his reins to a rusted-out bike rack. I palmed a peppermint to him and he nuzzled my hand. But when I moved to leave him, he let out a high whinny, a nervous sound, and blew air out his nostrils all forceful-like. I turned back.

The wind seemed to pick up just then, with a rumbling roll of thunder off in the distance. "I won't be long," I told Antique, and I caressed his nose. He let out a huff of air through his nostrils again. He wasn't pleased.

He didn't want me to go. Maybe he wanted a longer ride. Surely that's all it was. But it somehow seemed like more, like he was warning me off.

I ignored Antique, letting him humph and neigh and complain as I turned for the beach. The first of the storm's raindrops plummeted from the sky, and I picked up my pace, jogging toward Tempest.

It was still awfully early, so there were only a few other people on the thin strip of beach. A small redheaded kid wearing nothing but a pair of tighty-whities dug in a tidal pool at the water's edge, his mother sitting cross-legged not far from him. She waved hello absentmindedly as I hurried past.

An older couple with matching green windbreakers walked hand in hand toward the pier, their bare feet splashing in the tide. The woman pointed toward the horizon and the man's eyes followed, tracking the path of a pelican as it dove toward the water. They both pulled up their hoods against the gray drizzle.

I was running now, past these people, watching Tempest ahead of me. I could tell the moment that she realized I was there. She didn't turn around, but I could see it in her posture, feel her awareness inside my own. My flip-flops crunched against the black sand as I closed the gap between us.

Of course, the push between us was there.

The closer I got, the stronger it registered, until it felt almost like a concrete thing between us. When I was a few yards from my sister, it actually hurt. It wasn't just a little bother anymore. No, now it had moved fully into the territory of pain, producing a terrible pounding in my head, red and orange stars blooming in the edges of my vision. It was a gnawing kind of thing with teeth and claws, digging its way out of my skull from the inside.

Tempest turned now, her pigtails flapping into her face because of the wind. "Don't come any closer," she said.

We stood there, ten or fifteen feet away from each other. I shook my head against the pain of being near her. "Tempest. I'm fighting this."

I took another step toward her. I tasted iron. I'd bitten my tongue without realizing it, clamping my jaw against the throbbing. It unnerved me, this feeling. It grew from my skull, took root in my chest, prickled under my fingernails, and scratched against my eyelids. It made me want to turn away, to retreat, truly. But I had other ideas.

"Why is it so bad?" I said, aware now that I had to raise my voice above the crash of the wind and surf, the rhythmic pitter-patter of the raindrops.

"It's the black sand. I'll explain later. We really shouldn't be together right now. Not here. I think that—"

"You were right, Tempest. I got something."

Tempest nodded. "I heard. You saved that wolf pup?"

"Yeah."

"How?"

"I can't really put words to it. I reached out, and it's like I could *feel* him, Tempest."

"Huh." This seemed to hurt Tempest, somehow. She looked up at the darkening clouds, opened her palms to the rain. She looked so sad in that moment, like she was giving in to something. "People are too difficult?" she asked.

"What are you talking about?"

I took a step closer to her, but the force between us surged higher, threatening to burn my lungs like paper beneath my ribs. "Tempest," I gasped, my throat pinching. "I'm gonna beat this thing. Okay?"

"No. Don't come closer, Tally!" Her voice had a jagged edge to it. She seemed terrified, and that nearly undid me.

I was tired of this. Tired of letting this thing win. I would not wind up like our mother and Aunt Grania. I would not. Darn the moon!

"Maybe if we just push through. I can do it. Just break through this cycle, and you jus—" I pushed forward, and I had to close my eyes against the pressure. I was going to face it one way or another. No more running.

"Wait! Tally!"

I opened my eyes, and Tempest was digging into the endless pockets of her cargo shorts. She pulled out a strange, glinting, metallic thing. It was a wide bracelet of some sort. "This," she said, even as she was backing away. "It's going to help, but I'm just not ready yet." She took a few steps away from me, going deeper out into the bubbling surf, the tide rolling over her toes.

"I'm not going to let this thing do this to us, Tempest. I'm going to show it who's boss." I pressed forward again, tipping my shoulders into it, eyes screwed tight, jaw clenched.

"It's too much, Tally!" she cried.

But I didn't listen. I reached inside myself. I found that power that was terrifying me, whatever it was in me that had reached out and connected with Pork Chop. I sought it out and I pushed forward with it, against the wall of pain keeping my sister and me apart. I could beat this. I had to.

For us. I was through being scared, being tentative.

I opened my eyes a crack to see Tempest in front of me, her arms up in some kind of defensive posture, shielding her face, still with that metallic bracelet in her hand. She was knee-deep in the water now, looking terrified.

I hated this. I summoned all that was inside of me, and I pushed.

From the corner of my eye, I became aware of the water to my left, the ocean waves growing.

"No!" Tempest yelled.

Yes, I thought. *Tempest is just scared. But I'm going to beat this thing. I am stronger than this.*

I was aware then of a great surge. It came from inside me. Tempest held her head in her hands, still backing away. I pressed forward into the water, my vision turning blurry, exploding into stars.

And a great flash of power erupted between us, like lightning but not the same. It zapped me like a shock of static electricity and left sparks hovering in the air like fireflies.

A great loud clap of thunder deafened me momentarily. I took one step.

My vision dimmed, and I struggled for breath, my lungs hot. But still, I pushed, aware that I was screaming now as I bent my head into the force and took another step. Surely, I had the willpower to break through this thing. This is what Aunt Grania, what Mama, what we had never done—just pushed through it.

Beaten it.

I was Tally Jo Trimble. I would out-muscle anything.

I focused my mind to a pinpoint and I pushed.

Then there was a whooshing noise; I opened my eyes just in time to see a great wall of water, a wave of epic size, coiled above us. It reached up between my sister and me in a strange, twisted shape: like it was stretched tight between us. My concentration flagged and broke—and then the wave did too. Letting loose, crashing over us.

It swallowed me. It swallowed Tempest. I had a fleeting worry for the old couple down the beach and the little toddler in his underwear.

The wave took me under, turned me head over heels, choked the breath from me as I flailed. It held me down and I struggled, pushed and pulled by the force of the tide. I opened my eyes and saw nothing but darkness. I turned over, trying to tread water, only to be pushed deeper by another wave.

This time it rolled over me, pushed me to the bottom, the water moving over me like a blanket, a grave.

I started to panic for air. Which way was there light? I was disoriented.

There.

I found which way was up and swam toward the sun. Another wave broke—this one less wild, maybe. My head broke the surface and I gasped for a breath. Once I got one, I screamed. "Tempest!"

She'd been farther in the water than me. My stupid bravery. My moronic certainty. "Tempest!" I screamed again, struggling to keep my head above surface.

How had we gotten in so deep?

Another wave crashed, fresh and strong, over my head. I scanned the water. What had I done to my sister?

Her head broke the surface, so far out. I screamed her name again. "Tempest!"

"Tally!" she called, breathless, her voice barely reaching me over the rush of the tide and the near-constant thunder.

I stroked toward her once, twice. She struggled to stay up, the waves much bigger out where she was. And my chest pinched with the effort of swimming and the adrenaline surging in my veins. I kept my head above the waterline, and my eyes pinned on her. I couldn't lose sight of her. I had to get to her.

She went under. I watched that spot, fear spiking through me. After an agonizing minute she came back up. And in that moment, I saw that she had red smeared on her forehead. She was blinking it from her eyes.

Blood.

"Tempest!" I called. She flailed weakly.

I moved to swim toward her, and a look of horror passed over her face. She said something, but her voice was lost on the wind. Then she held up her hand in a gesture I understood: Stop.

I got it then.

Stop.

It was there, still, between us. A writhing, angry thing. I was pushing it closer to her when she was trying to swim.

I watched as she struggled again against a wave, and it took her under.

A rush of absolute helplessness flowed through me as I treaded water, staying just this far away from my injured sister. Was she exhausted? About to lose consciousness from hitting her head? Would she drown 'cause I couldn't get to her?

Her head bobbed up. But would it again, after the next wave? And what could I do, if my going closer only made it worse?

I turned toward shore, panicking, swimming away from Tempest as fast as I possibly could. I had to get help.

Before I realized what was happening, someone was swimming past me. Steady, serious strokes. "I got her."

"Digger," I said through terrified tears.

"I got her," he said. "Go."

I turned toward the shore, my chest burning with exhaustion and fear and sadness—but I had to get away from my sister.

It was all I could do.

17

My hair wasn't all the way dry yet. I'd changed my clothes in our pod, but I still smelled like salt water, and I couldn't quit shaking. Digger and I sat on the picnic table outside the Candy Wagon.

"Here, drink this," Digger said, handing me a root beer float. "Fat Sam says you need sugar to counteract all the adrenaline."

"You sure she's okay?"

"Fat Sam is taking care of her. She's fine."

"Thank you."

"Are you okay? You're trembling something fierce. You cold?"

I nodded. Digger took off his sweatshirt and I put it on over my T-shirt. But I kept shaking. I wasn't just cold. I was reliving those moments in the water, the terror I'd felt.

"You're lucky you didn't tie up Antique very well. His reins were loose. He just took off and came back to camp, like a rescue dog, for crikey's sake. The moment I saw him, I knew something wasn't right."

"What if you hadn't been there, Digger?"

"But I was there."

I shivered. "But—"

"Tally. It wasn't your fault—"

"Hey," I interrupted. "Here she comes." Tempest came walking up from the animal tent. I stood up from the picnic table and backed away.

She started talking, but I was barely listening, taking her in from head to toe, inventorying everything about her with my eyes. She was in one piece, alive. "The black sand is a lodestone," she was saying when I finally tuned in. "It's essentially a magnet, making what's between us worse. Like a trigger, or an amplifier."

She looks fine, I told myself, trying to calm the hummingbird beat of my heart. Really. Her pigtails were reset, her hair nearly dried. "But . . . the blood. You hit your head?"

"Yeah, one of the waves took me under hard. It's on my scalp. Just a scratch, really. Fat Sam put some kind of salve on it." She fingered a spot near the crown of her head.

I let out a deep breath, steadying myself. I stood twenty feet from my sister, resisting the impulse to go to her.

I watched her chest rise and fall. I wanted so badly to throw my arms around her.

But I couldn't.

She was alive. That was all that mattered.

I wanted to say something, to apologize, to let her know what it meant to me that she was okay. I opened my mouth, but nothing came out. My throat narrowed and my eyes burned.

I was going to cry.

Tempest's eyes widened and she looked away. I watched the muscles in her throat as she swallowed. She motioned toward Digger. "Your dad's not gonna tell Pa Charlie? About . . . any of this?"

Digger shook his head. "No. He bought the story that you slipped on the boardwalk, that Tally jumped in after you."

"That's good."

"Now, what's lodestone? Explain it again, so we know it's safe now," Digger said. "I think Tally's freaking out."

"That black sand is magnetite. It acts as a magnifier—it makes magnets more powerful, by a zillion times, I think. But we're okay now. Back here, away from the shore."

"You sure?" I asked.

"Yeah, it's fine." Her smile wobbled.

"It's not fine." My voice was strained. "If Digger hadn't showed up, how would I have gotten you out of the water? I couldn't go near you!" I put my head in my hands for a moment. When I looked up at Tempest, her eyes looked as wild as I felt.

"But that didn't happen, Tally."

"This time."

Tempest studied her hands. "I lost the cuff in the water though."

"Who cares about the cuff?" I said. "I nearly lost *you*." I thought of Aunt Grania then, and I began to understand. "This is why I can't—I won't—"

"You're going to lose me for real if we don't try, Tally. That's what you were doing. You were trying. I'm glad. I mean, I'm not mad at you."

"You should be."

She plopped down on the picnic table, and I could once again feel what was between us, now that we were closer. A rhythmic push of pressure, throbbing between us. It made me want to just turn and run. I took one step back, then another, nearing the Candy Wagon.

Tempest kept talking. "Actually I am mad, a little. Not 'cause you tried, but 'cause you were acting like the big hero again. I don't need a hero, Tally. We're in this together. Let's try and—"

I shook my head. "No."

"I don't need a savior. I need a sister. I need you to do this *with* me. Bend the spoon."

I stayed silent. I was so exhausted, and I couldn't stop shaking, my knees actually knocking against each other. I couldn't fight about this anymore. I wouldn't.

"It's okay," Tempest said, motioning me over. The smile on her face was trying too hard. She blinked a few too many times. "Come on," she called. "Really, we're fine as long as we're not on that black sand."

I took a few steps closer.

We were okay. For now.

How long did we have? A few days until our birthday. That was it.

I weighed the risk against the reward. Soon, I probably wouldn't be able to be near Tempest at all. I told myself to enjoy the moment.

I sat down across from Digger, keeping myself a good five or six feet from my sister. Even so, I felt the steady buzz between us. It settled in my sternum, tickled the back of my throat.

Molly-Mae came out with a platter of cheeseburgers, and we descended on them like a pack of starving wolf pups.

"Y'all been awfully quiet out here," she said to the lot of us. "Makes me wonder what kind of trouble you're planning."

"Just need some refueling," Digger said, but even Digger's face was tight and worried-looking. Molly-Mae walked back to the Candy Wagon, and on her way she passed Aunt Grania coming toward us from the animal tent. I watched Molly-Mae press a hand to our aunt's wrist, just for a second, right over her tattoo.

"Girls, we need to talk," Aunt Grania said, approaching the table.

I wondered, then, what she knew about our morning. What Fat Sam had maybe told her. And from across the table,

Tempest gave me a little shake of her head. I knew she meant not to confess what had just happened.

I wouldn't.

I mean, I knew Tempest probably just wanted more time to work on her cuff, or whatever. But I realized it didn't really matter what the grown-ups knew or didn't know. This thing was too big.

It wasn't going to stay secret, not for long.

And when it didn't? The grown-ups wouldn't be any more prepared to deal with it than we were. That was for sure.

"Y'all want me to leave?" Digger asked, standing to offer Aunt Grania his seat.

"No," I said quickly.

Our aunt sat down, and so did Digger. He scooted close to me, nudging my shoulder with his. And maybe it was just an accident, but it felt like he was telling me he was here for me.

Aunt Grania took a long time looking us over: Tempest eating her cheeseburger, me feeling too queasy to even take a bite. Then Aunt Grania sighed, like she was giving in to something. "What do you know about the tides?" she asked.

"A lot," Tempest said, juice from her cheeseburger dribbling down her chin. "They're controlled by the moon."

"The moon pulls on the earth and vice versa," Aunt Grania said. "There are a lot of unseen forces at play in the world around us. And what do you know about the magnets?"

"Supposedly they cure gray hair," I said, my voice a rasp.

Tempest chimed in. "Have two magnetic fields ever sort of . . . *kaboom?* Exploded or, say . . ." Tempest's voice lowered to barely a whisper, "like, caused a fire or anything?"

"First," Aunt Grania said, looking from my sister to me, "you have to tell me what's happened between you two. Anything scary?"

"Nothing too big," Tempest answered quickly. "Just the pressure between us."

I felt too raw to lie right now, so I stayed silent, studying the grain of the picnic table wood.

When I finally looked up, Aunt Grania was nodding slowly. She must've come to the decision that she believed Tempest, at least enough.

"When your mother and I were here, our last summer together, I was into astronomy—just one of my many obsessions. I had this kick-butt telescope that I brought along in the catch-all. I was constantly mapping constellations, and I was wanting to get a tattoo when I turned eighteen. I'd settled on either the constellation Gemini, or just a simple half-moon. I tried to convince your mother to get one too."

Digger and I exchanged a look, remembering the note we'd read on the back of the silhouette garland.

"That was before everything happened," Aunt Grania continued. "Back then, the moon was just part of a show that the night sky put on each night for me. It was just a pretty light through my telescope, you know? Not like now." She shook her head. "After everything happened, I got this tattoo so I wouldn't forget the danger of the moon. This is my reminder."

She held up her arm, showing us the phases of the moon that encircled her wrist. It was a pretty tattoo. So delicately drawn. But it was also threatening.

A countdown.

"It started slowly, between your mama and me, probably how it is with y'all now. Little things. First time I noticed anything out of whack was when she was braiding my hair for me, and the static electricity between us was off the charts, the hairs on my neck and arms standing straight-out and crackling."

"It got worse?" Tempest asked.

"Yes," Aunt Grania answered. "With the moon, every lunar cycle, it grew."

Tempest asked, "Do you know what a Flower Moon is?"

Aunt Grania nodded. "The Flower Moon is in the spring, every few years, a special full moon, when the moon orbits very close to earth. And its pull on the tides is at its strongest."

"It's coming up soon—the Flower Moon," Tempest said. "In a few days."

"It is." Aunt Grania eyed us then. "But you must have a while still. I mean, it's just started between you. Your mother and I had years of warning."

I nodded.

Tempest and I did not have years.

We had days.

We both knew it. The Greenly Curse was upon us, right now. Fast. Furious. The moon striking the tinder of what was between us.

"Was it a Flower Moon when whatever happened between you and Mama?" I asked.

"It was."

My stomach knotted in anticipation. Here was Mama's story. What I wanted to know so badly, what I'd hunted down for the last week with fervor. And now? Now, I almost didn't want to hear it.

"It had been coming for a while, sneaking up on us, like the tide on a sandbar." Aunt Grania's voice wasn't much more than a whisper.

"The night it happened, there was a big Flower Moon, round and orange like a ripe melon, sitting in the sky. It was so close to the earth, so large. Like something out of a space movie, you know?"

"My energy was strong, thumping through my veins that day. I registered it, heard it in my eardrums, like a plucked piano wire—a vibration, see? And I suppose Genevieve's was the same, but opposite. The bass line to my treble. You get the idea. Aunt Grania gestured toward Pa Charlie's fire pit. "It happened right around the carnival campfire."

Tempest and I exchanged a look.

"Your mother and I were just horsing around. We were trying to light the campfire for Pa Charlie. He used to have this metal spark lighter, where you just—"

"I've seen it," Tempest said. "I mean, I was playing around with it one time in his garage. It's just two pieces of metal that rub against a bit of flint to make a spark."

"Yes, exactly," Aunt Grania agreed. "Pa Charlie used to use it to light his pipe."

Tempest added, "Pa Charlie got real upset when he saw me with it. He grabbed it right out of my hands."

Aunt Grania nodded. "Pa always used these little chunks of cedar wood as kindling. I imagine he still does. Well, Genevieve was fussing with the kindling in the bottom of the fire pit. She had rolled up some newspapers as well, and I came along with the old-fashioned sparker." Aunt Grania became real still for a moment. This memory was a powerful one.

"I remember that I was kneeling right next to Genevieve. We were both leaning over the fire pit, our heads just a hairsbreadth away from each other, Genevieve adding more newspaper, me just about to click the sparker." Aunt Grania's breath shuddered. "We felt it, what was between us. It was harsh and building by then. I shouldn't have lit the sparker. I should've been more cautious." Grania's voice broke.

I watched Aunt Grania's face as she relived this, the guilt there. How many times had she made herself remember?

How many times would I remind myself of what had happened earlier on the beach? I would have to live with that. Just as Aunt Grania lived with this.

"I clicked the lighter again and again. I couldn't get it to take."

Aunt Grania's eyes shot to mine and quickly moved to Tempest's. Digger seemed to be holding his breath next to me.

"Our mama, your granny, came by with one of her quilts tucked up around her shoulders, and she bent over the kindling, just exactly between Genevieve and me. I can still see it in my mind's eye, the tilt of her head over the fire, the way her long, dark braid swung over her shoulder. Your granny reached over to grab the sparker from me, to show me how it was done. But I was too stubborn. So I quick clicked the lighter again, once, twice. On the third try, it took, producing the tiniest of sparks." Aunt Grania's voice trembled.

"What was between us—the power—it caught fire and erupted into an explosion. The force of it threw Genevieve and me away from each other. But it lit your granny's quilt right up. Full-on, crackling flames. And it was hurting her—" Aunt Grania stopped then, her voice catching in a sob.

"Pa Charlie came from out of nowhere and rolled her in the dirt, suffocating the flames, but not before it singed her braid, burning inches of her hair."

"But Granny was okay, right? Her hair grew back, and everyone was fine?" Tempest asked, fingering her scalp where she'd been injured in the water.

Aunt Grania shook her head, her voice a strangled whisper, "No. The left side of her neck was burned pretty badly. She had a terrible scar after that."

I remembered that scar, all puckered and shiny. I'd never known what it came from.

I could barely swallow around the knot in my throat.

I understood then. This thing—what we had—it was a weapon.

"We separated after that. We'd been building up to that explosion for years. It wasn't a surprise, I suppose. We—I—I had to keep my sister and my family safe. Right?" Aunt Grania gave us a sad smile.

"But maybe it would have waned with the lunar cycle?" Tempest asked, a hint of desperation in her voice. She was still looking for a loophole that didn't exist.

"It never waned, not after the Flower Moon. We tried . . ." Aunt Grania shook her head. "That last Flower Moon, when we were eighteen, it was like it broke the dam, pushed everything between us into the stratosphere. Multiplied everything between us. And it never, ever went back."

There it was.

Their story.

Aunt Grania was no coward. Mama was no coward. They just loved each other. They split up before this thing . . . before it could do worse.

Grania left to keep Mama safe. To keep her family safe.

That's why they agreed to live apart, because . . . they knew.

I knew now too.

I understood what I was up against, how wild and unruly this all was. I got it now. It wasn't something I could stand up against and power through.

And today, on that beach, I'd been so darn sure of myself. So reckless. I *hurt* Tempest. She had blood streaming down her forehead.

I could've done so much worse.

Finally I understood what the real enemy to my sister was. The enemy wasn't the moon. It wasn't the tide or the black sand, or an old-fashioned spark lighter, or a generations-long family curse.

The real enemy was me.

Aunt Grania went on. "I'm sorry to tell you all this, girls. But history repeats itself. In new, but similar ways. Your grandmother and her sister were near nineteen. Your mom and I were eighteen. That's the real family legacy, not just all these twin girls."

"Oh, Tally Jo." It was Tempest now, and her face was crumbling. None of this was a surprise, but it was just so hard to hear it said out loud.

Like a confirmation, a nail in our coffin.

I got up, and I moved toward Tempest without thinking. But when I got a few steps away, I remembered.

I couldn't comfort my sister. The push was still there.

I fought my tears out of sheer pride. Tempest tried but failed, her breath coming out in a little sob. Aunt Grania went to her, gathered her up in her arms. They sat down at the picnic table.

Right in that moment, watching my sister cry, hearing her ask Aunt Grania, "Why?" I desperately wished I could take back all of our hurts of the last year, get back my time with

Tempest. I had to blink my eyes hard and fast to keep my tears at bay, and fury and fear welled up inside me.

"You were lucky," I said to Aunt Grania. My voice was hard and serious. "You could've done so much worse."

You could've destroyed your most favorite person in the world.

"You're lucky you didn't kill anyone, actually," I said, meaning Aunt Grania, but meaning me too.

"Tally," Digger said, and his face was ashen. Tempest's lips were tight.

"You're right," Aunt Grania said, looking at me. And I could see I was stoking her pain. I didn't care. She got up slowly, gave us a nod, and left us to stew in all this terrible reality.

I needed to remember this moment: that I was a . . . a weapon. Heck, we weren't even at the Flower Moon yet, and I gave myself chills just remembering the wave poised above us earlier this morning. Mama and Aunt Grania's close call had been terrible, but nowhere near as enormous.

Still, Aunt Grania and Mama had had the sense to separate.

I thought of the innocent old couple in their green windbreakers on the black-sand shore, the toddler digging in the tidal pool in his tighty-whities. They had been fine, unaffected. But what if they hadn't been? What if they had been swept up in the wave? What if next time. . .?

"I'll start the new cuff tonight," Tempest said, breaking the thick silence in Aunt Grania's wake. She reached for my hand, but I jerked away, an unconscious reaction to the painful pressure of her fingers coming too close to mine. It was there, not just a pressure, but pain. Still growing.

It felt reckless not to tell our parents everything. To even stay near each other at all.

I had to give up on besting this thing. Before I hurt someone. Before I hurt Tempest again. Because I needed Tempest to be okay, more than I needed anything for myself.

And the hollow feeling in my breadbasket, it was new to me. Heavy and still, a weight that wouldn't budge, only expanding on each breath.

It was maybe the feeling of giving up.

18

Two days passed, and Tempest and I avoided each other. I slept in the animal tent, on a hay bale near Pork Chop, too afraid to let what was between my sister and me have free rein while we were asleep inside a little metal pod. It seemed too akin to tinder inside a box.

And I tried to think of how to say goodbye to my sister. How would I do it? When? I couldn't wait too long. And who should I tell? Mama or Daddy? Who would take the news better? Would they divorce, each of them taking one of us?

These were impossible questions. I put them off, but with our birthday and the Flower Moon looming only three days away, I knew I couldn't ignore them much longer.

Tempest spent her time working on her inventions. I spent mine avoiding her.

•

But the very next day, she caught me coming out of the bathroom, and she waved me toward a picnic table. "Tally, you have to come over here."

I hesitated, weighing what was in the air between us.

"Come on. Closer. We're okay right now."

I did as she said, carefully. The pressure itched at my eardrums, pushed against my eyelids in a jagged, unpredictable rhythm, but it was nowhere near like on the beach.

"This will repolarize you . . . or me. One of us."

Tempest sat down at the picnic table, once again strewn with all kinds of tech supplies. Some bigger equipment sat on the ground: jumper cables, a handsaw, and an ominous-looking, black suitcase.

Digger sat at the table already, eyeing us with interest. He held a light bulb in one hand and he absentmindedly kept touching its lead to a battery, the bulb lighting up and shutting off again and again with his motion.

"Hey," Digger said to me.

"Hey." I stood nervously near them, and I watched the light bulb flicker.

Tempest used tin snips to cut a smooth edge on a flat, copper-colored piece of metal about the size of a Pop-Tart. This was obviously the new copper cuff. The replacement for the one I'd made her lose in the surf.

"I think I've finally adjusted the mechanism correctly," she said.

Tempest pressed a small, modified watch-like contraption into the middle of the metal sheet, laid what looked like a series of magnets attached to small disc batteries at the opposite end, and then she folded the metal sheet over, closing it up. In a few quick movements, she used pliers to press the rough edge over. Then she picked a tiny hammer out of her tool apron. She used it to pound the edges smooth, leaving a metal band, about two-and-a-half inches wide, with the little contraption and magnets hidden inside. She lifted it up, looking pleased, and then with some more hammering, she bent it into the form of a bracelet. "You've got to wear this," she said, handing me the cuff. "I just have to add the clasp."

"But what—"

"Put it on." I took the thing from her, feeling the pressure surge between us when I reached my hand out to her. Digger's light bulb grew bright and began to buzz in a strange, insect-like way.

I slipped the cuff over my hand. It was cool and smooth.

"Here," she said, definitively, shooing my hands away. Digger's light bulb grew brighter still, and then with a strange puff and click, it burned right out.

Digger jumped up and pulled the lead from the battery, and at the same time I jerked away from Tempest. But she held tight to me.

"Stop. That's nothing," she mumbled. She peered closely at the inside of my wrist, made some kind of measurements, and marked something on the copper cuff with a black marker. Then she took it off me again. "Not quite. It's got to fit perfect-like, really hug your skin." She put on a pair of safety goggles. "Stand back." She reached down to the black suitcase on the ground, fiddling with the metal closures.

Tempest stood up and produced a real, God-fearing blow-torch. "Holy smokes!" I yelped. "Who let you get ahold of that?"

But Tempest paid me no mind, firing the thing up like she'd been doing it for years. She stuck out her tongue in concentration just like our Daddy often does, and she got to work melding something to the copper cuff. "I mean, what's the tide other than just a big push and pull, you know?" she said. "The moon pulls on the earth; the sea responds. There you go: tides."

"Okay."

"The earth and the moon, they dance. We need to dance again." Tempest smiled like that explained everything. "It's like I was supposed to lose that first cuff in the sea. You did me a favor, Tally. This one's better. It's gonna work."

She handed Digger the cuff, then he handed it to me. The metal still felt warm from being under the heat of the blow-torch. I peered at the fancy new eyehook fasteners.

"Put it on," she said. "Digger, help her."

I did as I was told, slipping it over my wrist, and it fit right against my skin, conforming exactly to the shape of my wrist and arm. I fumbled with the fasteners, until Digger grabbed my arm to close them up himself. It wasn't instantaneous, but the air around me calmed, little by little. I felt it in my eardrums first, lessening, pulling back by degrees. Eventually I took a big breath, only then aware how thin the air had been before. I settled onto the bench of the picnic table across from Tempest, and Digger sat by my side. My sister and I stared at each other for a while, exhausted.

I thought of Tempest asking me on the Ferris wheel why I didn't trust her, didn't believe in her.

"I'm going to have to work on it again. It's not perfect. We might need more . . . power in it."

"I can really feel the difference." I couldn't quite let myself admit it, but it was true. I wasn't just imagining it. "It's working," I told her. "It really is."

"Switches the poles," Tempest said.

Dear God, Tempest was saving us. Better not to look at it head-on, better not to question it. Better not to let hope rear its ugly head.

So I let this weird, new calm settle between my sister and me, and I watched Digger. He was playing with a roll of the thinnest copper wire, and in front of him sat a couple of animals he'd made. He'd gotten better since the dragonfly. He had a butterfly, a jellyfish, and a beetle lined up on the table, and they looked so lifelike, with this perfect sense of motion to them. Now, he sat working on a new one: what looked like a tiny bird. There was something calming in watching him coil the wire, snip it, and bend it just so. The tiny sparrow had such a pleasing little form when Digger finished and sat him up on the little round table, his wings up behind him like he was just about to take flight.

Digger started on another creature, something a little smaller. I tried to make out the outline of the thing, but Digger was taking his time, and it looked like just a series of intertwining circles. But then he got far enough into it, and I realized: a starfish!

At that moment, something slipped into my mind, sharp and clear, and I knew immediately that it had come from Tempest.

It wasn't a thought really, not an image, but an impression. A nudge, like when she had stopped me from punching Bradley Ballard.

I looked across the table, and I saw my sister. I tried to open my mind to her. To this thing between us, this *change*. And I asked myself if I believed in Tempest's wrist-cuff gadget enough to delve inside myself again, to find my own magic, to test it out.

I'd promised myself I wouldn't. It was too scary. Too unwieldy.

I watched Tempest.

She eyed Digger's copper animals.

I could tell what she was trying to do. I knew.

It wasn't working though.

She couldn't do it herself. She wanted me to help. She wanted me to try.

Tempest could build a liar gauge. She could reassemble a car engine. She could darn near bend a spoon with her mind.

And she could create this wrist cuff that could make us sitting in tight proximity pretty darn comfortable.

But she couldn't do what she was trying to, right now. No, she needed my help. And I was too scared to give it.

I had put the cork on what was inside me. And I didn't want to—no, I couldn't—let it loose again. We had come very close to something very bad on that beach, something worse than us being separated.

Then there was just one word in my mind: Please?

I looked into Tempest's face the way she was trying so hard to smile at me, to give me that, even when everything was going down the drain. Tempest had built this cuff for me. She had stolen for us, at the very least, some more time.

It's only a couple copper bugs, I told myself. *It isn't half the ocean suspended above your sister's head.*

I was worrying about hurting my sister, or someone else. And I knew, as my heart thumped a hard, guilty beat against my ribs, that I would always and forever be worrying about that, every moment of every day, until the dreaded horrible moment when we were separated. For good.

But for now, I was going to risk it.

Because I believed in my sister. I had to.

She asked me to trust her, and I was going to do it.

I concentrated on the butterfly. I found that writhing thing inside me, the magic that so badly wanted to be let loose, and I slipped the lid off, just a tad.

Then, Tempest's voice was in my head again. I need you with me, Tally.

I got what she meant. I looked for her. Her energy. Like I had with Pork Chop.

What if this, what was inside me—what if I could do this *with* my sister?

It seemed so simple. It really did. But it was a revelation to me—the strong one, the leader, the brave warrior.

I could share the power.

I closed my eyes, dug deep inside myself, harnessed the slip of magic I'd let loose, and searched for Tempest's force.

I reached out for my sister's energy, and I found it, with the same wash of warmth I'd felt when I connected with Pork Chop. I had latched on to Tempest's energy somehow—my will weaving together with hers. My . . . whatever. Maybe it didn't even need words.

Maybe we didn't have words for it yet.

We're in this together.

I watched the copper-wire butterfly shake a little bit. Just the tiniest, nearly imperceptible wobble.

"You can do it," Tempest said.

"*We* can do it." That was the difference, right there. We. I tried once more. The butterfly trembled, and it flopped onto its side. "We have to work it together," I said.

"I'll take the top. You take the bottom. We'll sort of push against each other," she said. And for once, I let her take the lead. And it was scary and it was weird. It wasn't the way I usually went about things. But it worked.

We both concentrated. I made the front of my brain just sort of shut off—I couldn't ask how or why right then. I knew that would kill it, whatever was taking root and coming alive. So I let those questions lie.

The little butterfly shook again, and I heard a gasp from Tempest as it lifted off the grimy picnic table, just an inch or so. But then I took a deep breath, and I pushed it with my mind. Up.

And Tempest pushed it down. Together we kept it suspended, just like that poor old frog in the science lab. Levitating. Magnetic fields, opposing poles. That, my mind understood; but how we got that butterfly to move—to really fly, not just hang there like a shaky marionette . . . I didn't know. I didn't care.

I let it fly. Tempest and I worked together, anticipating each other's moves. Making that butterfly soar and swoop. Climb high and dive low.

"Do another," Digger said, his eyes wide as golden dollars.

Keep that one up, I told Tempest. But I didn't use my mouth. I used my mind. I held the butterfly with Tempest, with my brainpower, but then I turned toward the dragonfly too.

I pushed it up. Tempest joined me, our forces working together, opposite but together. Equals.

But just when the dragonfly began to move steadily, the butterfly fell with a crash that scared us both.

The dragonfly clattered to the ground too, and we giggled as we tried again. And again. And then some more. Until we could do it.

Two at a time, with different flight patterns, separating our focus. We had almost all the animals flying figure eights over the table, while Digger got busy coiling more wire. "I don't know," I said, as I tried to help Tempest keep the first two up at the same time I got the sparrow started. It was heavier in general.

But Digger quickly made another butterfly and a second dragonfly, and pretty soon the area around us was full of tiny, flying copper creatures. Six of them. Tempest and I had them all going, our forces pulling and pushing. The invisible cords of communication between us wrapped tight around each other, amplifying our power, making things possible. Boosting our magnetic force. Whatever we were doing, it was only because it was both of us.

Tempest and I had just launched the seventh little animal—a bumblebee—into the air when we heard a voice.

"My God."

The magic, or whatever had pushed the force of the air underneath those tiny copper wings, disintegrated into nothing in the blink of an eye. And the animals fell, all seven of them, one of the beaks hitting me square on the nose. "Ouch."

"Aunt Grania," Tempest said. She looked to me for help explaining.

"How in the world can you girls do that?" Aunt Grania asked, and I didn't like the look on her face, which was something other than just awe or wonder. There was fear.

I answered her with a shrug, gave her a smile.

"We're working together," Tempest answered.

I had this energy pushing out from the center of me, making me brave and alive. I knew we could do this. I didn't want to stop.

But just then, I had a flash of that wave, that moment on the beach. When I was darn near pulling the whole ocean toward us.

I shivered in fear. What was I doing playing around with this power?

Aunt Grania narrowed her eyes at me, and she looked just as stubborn as Mama in that moment. "What you two have, it's bigger, more powerful than anything your mama and I had. You need to be more careful. This is . . . scary."

"We have Tempest though. She's a genius." I held up my wrist, showing Aunt Grania the cuff, feigning confidence.

I watched Aunt Grania grimace and the last of that light feeling in my chest just sort of flittered off into the air.

I saw the cuff for what it was, what it looked like. And I doubted us. Was this flimsy piece of metal really all that was keeping Tempest and me from . . . what?

Blowing up?

Crackling into flames?

Or worse, living apart?

And my mind replayed the scene at the beach earlier—what could've happened, what nearly did happen. I felt suddenly silly and naïve.

What were we playing at?

19

Fat Sam came walking up just then, a worried look to his brow. "There's somebody out yonder looking for y'all."

"For who?"

"He's up near the ticket booth. Asking for the Numbers Girl."

I followed Tempest toward her rickety old card table near the midway, oblivious to the buzz and noise of the carnival.

It was turning toward night now, and the nearly full moon hung large in the cloudless sky. Shining and sleek, yellow against a black sky, the edges fuzzy with clouds. How could something so beautiful be so threatening?

In two days, Tempest and I would be thirteen. The Flower Moon would be upon us, its powerful pull at its peak.

And . . . what then?

Suddenly, I was struggling for breath. I couldn't relax and my throat tightened. I took two puffs of my inhaler, but it didn't help much.

It was already getting dark, and the lights strung up around the midway swung in the breeze, casting little shadows that danced around us as we approached Tempest's card table. A man who appeared to be older than God sat next to Tempest's table in an aluminum lawn chair. His walker, complete with those goofy tennis balls on the ends, stood next to him, a bit askew, as if he'd sat down in a hurry.

Digger approached him first, and he held out his hand to shake. "Good evening, sir." The man shook it, not getting up, his eyes working from Tempest to me and back again.

"We're twins," Tempest said to him, gesturing toward me.

"I guess so," he answered, his yellowed teeth appearing in a surprisingly tender smile behind his ancient lips. Tempest gave that old man a good looking-at, but she shook her head. "I'm not getting anything, sir. My number radar is not absolute."

"Oh, it's not me who's wanting to see you. It's my grand-baby." As if conjured, a little girl, maybe six or seven, came running up with her bag of popcorn, her right front tooth missing.

"She's here!" she said, eyeing Tempest and me. "There's two of them!" she exclaimed, her head whipping back and forth to look at both of us.

"I'm the Numbers Girl," Tempest said.

"Scarlett here is obsessed with numbers," the old man said, repositioning the tubes that went into his nose. That's when I noticed the oxygen tank that he held in a cotton-patterned sling over his arm. His breath wheezed in and out as he mussed the little girl's hair affectionately. "Scarlett heard about you down at the pier, and I just had to bring her to meet you."

"I do Sudoku and math puzzles, jigsaws and sequences. Do you?" the little girl said.

"Sometimes," Tempest answered. "I like all kinds of brain teasers." Tempest was looking at her hard, and I noticed the dark smudges underneath Tempest's eyes. How rough had the past few days been on my sister? Making this cuff. The whole fiasco at the beach. Fighting what was between us.

Tempest pushed against her temples with her fingers, then sighed. "I'm sorry. I'm just not getting anything. Usually, I get a . . . well, a flash of knowing, or something, but—"

She stopped and looked at me. "It's you, Tally. You're jamming me."

"I am?" I backed away.

"Could we try together?" she asked.

"No, I don't think—"

"You know, I think this is all meant," she motioned from her to me and back again, her voice now a whisper. "This is all meant for us to do together. That's why, I think, the beach was such a disaster—"

"Give me a second," I said. I knew she was right. I did.

I pressed my hand to the cuff on my wrist.

Was I going to trust this?

What Tempest and I had done with Digger's flying creatures . . . I don't know. It had seemed so hopeful.

"Okay," I said, finally. "Together."

Tempest smiled. She closed her eyes.

A small crowd had assembled around us by now—a knot
of carnival-goers and workers alike. I took a deep breath and
closed my eyes too. I felt the thrum of my sister's energy working in the air around us. I took a step forward, like it was
sucking me in.

I held on to the metal cuff at my wrist.

"You're both in on this, huh?" the old man asked. My eyes
popped open and Tempest was watching me.

"Well, we're kind of a team," Tempest explained. "Like the
earth and the moon."

Tempest fixed the little girl with a stare. I searched for
Tempest's energy.

My power met hers, and they intertwined, coiled
together . . .They thrummed, beat a rhythm together. They
existed on their own, but when they joined, they morphed into
something wild.

But I couldn't get scared now. That wasn't what my sister
needed.

I concentrated, letting my eyes close, and I could feel this
buzzing, like an electric toothbrush, on my wrist cuff, the
vibration traveling up the length of my arm.

Just reach out, Tempest said in my mind. Reach out.

I did like she told me. I listened with my energy, let it combine with Tempest's, and we reached out. Together.

It came to me in a jolt, as if I was waking from a nightmare. A number. A date.

November 3rd.

I said it out loud, and I looked to Tempest. She was smiling wide, all triumphant-like. She had felt it too.

But then I looked at the girl, and her nose wrinkled. Something wasn't right. Something felt off.

November 3rd. It wasn't the girl's number.

No, it wasn't going to mean anything to her. I'd gotten my wires crossed somehow.

Because suddenly I knew what November 3rd meant, clear as a June Georgia sky.

I turned around to see Digger standing right behind me. Surely he'd been peering over my shoulder the whole time. He stared at me now.

November 3rd.

Digger. All hopeful eyes and supportive smiles.

My Digger.

My dear, favorite friend, whose parents were divorcing. Digger, who'd been hurting all summer long, hoping for something that was never gonna happen. Did he know?

Did he suspect?

When I met his stare, I tried to shutter my gaze before he saw, but his eyes widened for a moment.

In that second, I think he knew; he sensed the date had something to do with him.

"What is it, Tally?" Digger asked. His face fell, and he let out this nervous chuckle. "Really, just tell me. You're kinda freaking me out."

I took another step toward him. I started to say something, wanted to say anything comforting.

November 3rd.

I couldn't find the words.

"Tally, you don't get to throw something like that out and then look at me all panic-eyed and not explain yourself."

"What is it, Grandpa?" the girl asked from behind me.

"I'm sorry, kiddo," Tempest explained, "but this thing is not a perfect science, and we aren't getting a number for you today."

"Aw, no fair," she grumbled, and then her old grandpa stood up with his walker and shuffled away with her. Tempest followed them, trying to make it up to the little girl with a trip to the Candy Wagon. I wanted to follow them, to get out from under Digger's gaze. I took a step or two backward, but then Digger stopped me with a hand on my shoulder.

"Hey."

And in that moment, with Digger's hand on my shoulder, the connection sparked clearer in my mind, and I *saw* it.

I didn't want to see it.

The slow-moving image of Digger's smiling mother, her red hair pushed up into a knot, held together by fancy pearl barrettes. The blue-and-white, stained glass windows of the church glowing with sunlight. The balding man standing next to her in a blue three-piece suit.

November 3rd.

Digger's mother was getting remarried.

There wasn't going to be any reunion between his mom and Fat Sam. She was going to marry this other guy, and Digger's heart was going to crack because of it, all his hopes lost.

And he knew this now because of me.

Digger's eyes went wide.

"You saw it too?" I asked, but I already knew the answer. Digger nodded once, slow and sad. I reached for my inhaler, my lungs squeaking around a breath. "I'm so sorry, Digger."

"Tally . . ."

"November third," Tempest said, joining us again, and I hated the sound of the words as they hung in the air.

All I ever wanted to do was protect the people I loved. Why couldn't I ever manage to do it?

"It's just a shock, is all," Digger said.

"We could be wrong," Tempest offered.

"Yeah," Digger said, but his eyes were wet, his shoulders slumped, and I hated everything and everyone in that moment.

The crowd around us was dissipating, with low murmurs and suspicious glances toward Tempest and me.

I swallowed hard through the pinhole my throat seemed to have become.

I took two more puffs from my inhaler.

"Tally." It was Tempest's voice, low and worried, her hand coming up to touch my elbow.

I jerked it away.

"I think I'm done here," I said, not looking at her.

I turned and stalked off down the midway. But as I made my way past Tempest, something buzzed and crackled on my wrist, and suddenly, whatever the cuff had been doing, it didn't do it anymore. A near explosion of pressure pushed me away from my sister, in a force so large that my feet lifted off the ground. I sailed back onto my butt, skidding to a halt on the gravelly midway.

The air flew out of my lungs.

"Tally!" Digger said, coming to my aid, but I shoved him away. I couldn't get a breath.

I saw Tempest across the midway from me, on her rump as well. She rubbed at her shoulder like she'd hit it when she landed.

I found my voice, struggling to stand up. Suddenly so angry. "What did we think? This was going to solve it? Nothing's solved!" I ripped that cuff from my wrist and threw it on the ground near Tempest. As soon as I got my feet under me, I took off running.

I didn't listen to my sister calling after me. I didn't wipe the tears from my cheeks. I didn't do anything but get myself away.

I tripped on some litter on the midway and nearly fell face-first in the gravel. Digger had chased after me, of course, and now he tried to help me up. I shook him off. "Leave me alone," I barked.

I ran all the way down the midway and past the crabgrass field, toward the abandoned airplane hangar.

I wanted to go home. I wanted Mama. And Daddy. I wanted to go back to Atlanta, to Bones and his fleas, to not knowing anything about anything. I just wanted to be a regular kid.

I kept walking, over the unused airstrip, and past that even, toward the stand of peeling birches and their canopy of kudzu.

It wasn't until I was there and I had plopped on the ground that I truly began to sob, shoulders shaking, chest heaving. "Son of a monkey's uncle," I barked at myself, wiping at those silly tears. "Grow up, Tally!"

I sat there for a long time, and then I reclined onto my elbows, spotting the shining stars through the trees, trying to focus my thoughts on only the song of the cicadas, the accompanying harmony of the frogs.

The moon in all its near-full glory shone above me, so large and powerful, mocking me and my sorrows.

I stood up and cursed at that moon, raised my clenched fists at it. Said every bad swear I'd learned from Arnie and Hames and the rest of the carnies. I found some rocks in the dirt, and I threw them stupidly up at the moon, watched them do nothing but arc into the air and fall helplessly back to earth.

I collapsed into a heap on the ground.

I pulled my knees to my chest and let my head fall against them. I took deep breaths for a long time, finally calming my lungs down.

Eventually, I lay back onto the grass, exhausted. I swatted at the mosquitoes and no-see-ums, but other than that, I just lay still, the earth cool and calming beneath me. The rhythmic swaying of the Spanish moss on the branches above my head comforted me somehow.

And I thought about Mama and the secret sadness behind her eyes, about Aunt Grania, about this strange sisterly curse, and about the power I'd just felt between my sister and me.

I thought about our birthday, about what more could possibly be coming our way. And I heaved a great big sigh.

I plucked a few blades of the grass beneath me and chewed on them. They tasted bitter.

What was it all for anyway? Digger's Mom. Pork Chop's rusty nail. What was this power—this curse—good for anyway?

"I give up," I whispered into the night.

"No, you don't."

I opened my eyes. Digger stood over me, blocking out the light of the moon. But then he moved, sitting down in front of me, cross-legged.

"The Tally I know has more fight in her than that." He reached for my hand, pulled me to a sitting position.

And then I couldn't get my apology out fast enough. "I'm sorry I was so mean to you down at the graveyard. I'm sorry about your parents splitting up. I'm sorry I never said anything before now. I really am, Digger."

"I know, Tally." He let go of my hand and stretched his legs out in front of him, all long limbs and easy smile.

"How are you? You okay?"

Digger smiled. "I'm all right, Tally Jo." He brushed me off in his usual, laid-back, Digger way, but I could tell it meant something to him, that I was talking to him about all this. Finally.

"And I'm real sorry about just now. Your mom remarrying. And I—"

"Tally, none of that is your fault. And it'll be fine. I mean, I want my mom to be happy. And I think I kind of already knew there was no chance . . ." He gave me his Digger smile then, all full of mischief and easy optimism. "But I'm a dreamer, you know?"

I nodded. I did know that.

"You okay?" he asked me.

That was Digger Swanson. I had just ruined his dreams of his parents getting back together, and he was asking me if I was okay. And I was going to answer him honestly.

"No, I'm not." I pinched at the bridge of my nose. "Why do you put up with me, Digger?"

"You telling me all this time I've had a choice?"

I smiled. I even laughed a little, though I didn't want to. I looked up at the sky, pointed toward the moon. "It's darn near full."

"Yeah. Two days."

"It'll be at its most powerful."

"You're powerful. Even more powerful than the moon, I'd wager."

"How?" I sputtered. "Powerful, like I can tell my very best friend some terrible news that he surely could've waited for? I mean, what is this all for?" I ripped some grass out of the ground and threw it up in the air. "What's this all for, Digger, huh? You tell me that."

Digger gave me another Digger smile, this one thoughtful and a bit sly. "What's any of this for?" He motioned to the sky, the world around us. He shrugged.

"That's all you got?"

"Yeah, that's all I got." He leaned forward though, like he was letting me in on a secret. "But who knows what you could do, Tally Jo? Don't you want to find out?"

I pulled my knees back to my chest, held them there, pressed against the emptiness in my breadbasket.

"I don't know. It's scary. I get it now, why Mama and Aunt Grania—"

"Oh, I see. You're chicken."

"Digger—"

"Squawk, squawk," he teased, flapping his arms like a chicken, then elbowing me a bit.

He expected me to argue. Instead I felt tears prick at my eyes again. "I just—" My voice caught and I had to fight a sob. I pressed my hands over my face.

"Hey, hey," he said, scooting closer, throwing an arm over my shoulder. "Jeez, Tally, I'm sorry. I didn't mean it. I was just teasing. I didn't mean anything."

I waved it away. "It just . . . everything feels enormous, Digger. Huger than me. I don't know if I can do it. I *am* chicken. I'm scared of hurting my sister, or somebody else."

"I believe in you, Tally."

I rolled my eyes.

"No. Listen. You don't have to use this thing—you really don't. You can look it in the face and conquer it, wear that cuff and stick by your sister. You don't have to do any more flying bugs or looking into the future. For real, you don't. But . . . I don't know. To me, it seems a little quick just to give up on all that magic."

"I don't know, Digger."

Digger pulled up a blade of grass and chewed on it himself. He gave me a bit of the side-eye. I knew there was something else.

"What?" I said.

"Tally, your mama will be here soon. She'll know what's going on. And she's going to separate y'all. She'll feel it between y'all, fairly thrumming."

"I know."

"Maybe Tempest can fix up that cuff right quick. Maybe things can go right back to somewhat normal between you two."

"I'm not ever gonna be normal again."

Digger sighed. He took his arm from my shoulders. Then he leaned over and took one of my hands between both of his.

He waited until I met his eyes. "Don't you get it, Tally? That right there."

"What?"

"Normal. You want to be normal? You don't see it. But I see it." He chuckled. "Whether you're making copper wires fly, or speaking to wolf pups, or . . . not. No matter what. To me, Tally Jo, you've always been magic."

Digger.

Suddenly, I couldn't meet his eyes.

What he said, it did something to my heart. It felt like he broke it in two jagged halves and healed it all at once.

"What exactly are you scared of, Tally Jo?" He squeezed my hand in his.

I squeezed it right back. Then I confessed, my voice nothing but a whisper, "I'm scared of not living up to what you seem to think I can be. Of letting everyone down."

"Impossible. Not in your nature."

And when I finally got the courage to peer up at Digger, the look in his eyes . . . it was so warm, so knowing, I wanted to curl myself up and live inside the way he was looking at me. Forever.

I sighed. Digger had a way of making me want to be the best version of myself. "Digger, how long can Tempest and I go on with something like this. Something that we don't truly understand?"

"There are lots of things we don't understand in the world, Tally."

"Like?"

Digger scratched at the back of his neck, thinking. "What about people who lift whole cars to save a loved one? Or Bigfoot sightings? The pyramids?"

I laughed in spite of myself. "Those are different kinds of things."

"Are they? I think they're the same. It's a Flower Moon, Tally Jo. I think some things—great things, awesome things—only come around once in a long while, and you gotta snatch 'em up. Hold them close. 'Cause you won't get anything quite that rare and special again anytime soon. Like the Flower Moon. Like the fun we have at the carnival every summer." His voice dropped. "Like the kind of friend you are to me." He yanked on some grass then, studied it closely.

"You've always been the most fun part of my summers, Digger. You know that, right?" And right then, watching the magical way the moon lit up Digger's profile, watching the way a smile played at the corner of his lips, I realized something.

What was happening between Tempest and me, all of it—the magnets and poles, power and electrical charges—was science that just didn't have an explanation yet. But it would. Equations would be solved, hypotheses proven.

But what was between Digger and me, the feeling welling in my heart, the love I had for him, for this ramshackle carnival, for my dear, dear sister . . . that was magic.

Maybe that was what growing up was, understanding where the real magic lived in this world. Inside our very own hearts.

Learning to hold on to it. Cherishing it.

Because that was another thing about growing up: you realized there wasn't anything you could do about some things. Terrible things, awful things were going to happen: Digger's parents' divorce, my granny passing before I really got to know her, Mary Anning dying out by the chicken coop. All those things were coming for us; no one was getting out of here without a little of that pain.

You couldn't stop these things.

But you could be there for each other in those moments. There was magic in making sure that the people you loved never had to feel alone in any of it. Magic in holding someone's hand through the pain, healing their hearts with a kind word, or soothing with a soft smile.

Wasn't there?

"Come on," I said, standing up and offering Digger my hand.

"Where're we going?"

"Well," I said, pulling Digger up from the ground. "First things first. We have to get Tempest to make Aunt Grania a bracelet."

20

Digger sat next to me on my bed, following Tempest's instructions. "You gotta hook it as tightly as it will go," she told him.

Digger fumbled with the new wrist cuff on my arm. Tempest let out an annoyed sigh from her perch just outside the door of our pod, our tiny trailer full and pulsing with pressure. She didn't dare come any closer—not yet, anyway. We had to get the new cuff working first.

"There," Digger said, finally catching the latch and pulling the two halves closed. It settled onto my wrist, and if anything it was lighter, but more tightly fitted, than the last one. I felt the throbbing around us dwindle.

I took a good, deep breath. "It works."

"I knew it would." Tempest pulled on her eyelashes as she stepped into the pod.

"Okay. What exactly does it do again?"

"Reverses the polarity. So we can be together. Attract, not repel."

"How?"

"I don't know the exact science of it. Not yet. "

"And you're okay with that?"

Tempest shrugged. "The real question is, are we going to try and doing anything with what we've got, Tally?"

"Hey, I think I can give this cuff a second chance," I said. "But I don't know about flying those bugs around, or—" Digger had stood up and was drifting toward the door. "Don't you dare leave, Digger Swanson," I told him.

"You two have a lot to talk about, Tally Jo."

"I need someone on my side, Digger."

"Then I better leave, because you already know I agree with Tempest."

I glared at him. "You're right. You should leave."

Digger leaned on the doorjamb. "Tally, you can't be scared to try again. Are you going to spend your life wondering what would have happened if you'd given y'all a second chance? Like when I pitched against Thornton Middle School last year, I never got the chance to—"

"I said leave, Digger! You aren't helping my cause."

Digger shook his head and left, the screen door to our pod clanging loudly behind him.

I turned toward my sister.

She sat on her bed across from me. "I still can feel it, you know," I told her.

"I know."

"We're learning how to deal though."

Tempest smiled at me. "We are."

My sister. Tempest.

"You think the cuff stopped working last night because I quit, you know . . . *believing* in it?" I asked her.

Tempest considered this. "Is some of this ruled by emotions? I don't know, maybe. Probably. But, Tally, that's easily fixed. Just do me a favor and believe in it, okay?"

"Got it. Will do."

"Good." Tempest eyed me like she wasn't sure I could do it. I wasn't sure either.

"On the beach," I said. "What almost happened . . . That really scared me."

"I know. But that wasn't *us*."

"No, I know—"

"It was you."

"Yeah. I was trying to do it all, just overriding you, and . . . I'm sorry, Tempest."

"Don't. That's over. We know how to work together now. It'll only get better. And—"

"Is that what it's always been like?" I asked, my voice a whisper. "Me bossing you, never—"

"Tally, no. For a very long time, I needed you to do that for me. I needed you. And I still do—just in a different way."

"You don't need me being the protector, trying to fix things."

"I need you on my side."

"I'm sorry I didn't tell you about Mary Anning. I kept you from being with her when she died. I was wrong."

"It's okay, Tally." Tempest pulled a few of Digger's copper bugs from her pocket. "I was thinking. Maybe if we—"

I shook my head. "Why can't we just—"

"Go back to how we were?"

"No. That's not what I was going to say. Just maybe . . . maybe we should just be glad that we can be near each other."

"Remember in kindergarten," she said, giving me a look, "the mirror in the bathroom?"

"Of course I remember."

"I was so afraid of being without you. I was scared to death, but every morning, when my class would go to bathroom break, I'd find a little note taped to the mirror. A picture, a word or two. Always from you."

"My class had bathroom break first so I would just—"

"Growing up, you taught me how to believe in myself, Tally. How to be strong."

"Oh, come on now. I just—"

"Don't make light of it. You did. But now I'm asking you to believe *in us*. Okay?"

I wanted to agree. I did.

"Think about it."

I nodded, lifted up my wrist cuff. "Should we keep a safe distance between us tomorrow?" I asked my sister. "It's our birthday, and the Flower Moon, and all."

Tempest threw up her arms. "I don't know, Tally. It's hard to know. I'll tell you what—either that, or we never leave each other's side. Stick together like glue."

"Well, either way, we'll face tomorrow together," I said, trying not to sound scared.

"We're going to face everything together, from now on," she said, and she reached across the small space between our beds and grabbed my hand. I flinched, afraid of what would happen. Nothing did.

I grabbed her hand right back.

It was such a simple thing: my sister's palm against my own. How many times had we held hands growing up? Hundreds? Thousands? But right then, I didn't take it for granted.

And seeing Tempest take that chance, reaching for my hand—well, it had filled me with hope. It made me want to be brave.

21

I still didn't sleep in the pod with my sister. Even with the cuff, it felt too dangerous. I nestled down on a bale of hay in the animal tent, and the next morning I woke with a start, startling Pork Chop from my lap. He let out a little bark of displeasure when he tumbled to the floor of the stall.

And that's when Digger walked in, banging on one of Molly-Mae's kitchen pots with a giant wooden spoon. "Happy birthday to you!" he sang, his rhythm all off. And, jeez, he had an off-key voice, like Bones trying to howl with the coyotes.

Pork Chop growled at Digger's singing. So did I.

"Get up, you lazy bones!" Digger said.

"I'm awake." I rubbed at my eyes.

"Let's go get your sister. Molly-Mae made Tempest's favorite French toast for her birthday breakfast. I love that stuff, smothering it with syrup and powdered sugar."

"Oh, okay," I grumped.

"And of course she's frying you up some hash browns." He chuckled then, like he knew that was what I was waiting for.

"Now you're talking." I stood and stretched, finally smiling.

So it was official. Tempest and I were thirteen years old.

We spent a lot of the morning around each other, at breakfast and after, fielding hugs and birthday wishes from the rest of our carnival family. The air was fairly churning around us. I felt it, and I'm sure Tempest did too. And Digger. Probably everyone. My sister and I crackled every time we came within a few yards of each other, even with me wearing my wrist cuff. But it was bearable. It was. For now.

The Flower Moon would be full tonight, high and glowing in the sky, pulling all our power to the surface.

For sure, something was gathering up steam, coming for us.

We just didn't know what *it* was, exactly.

Tomorrow the carnival would be loading up and moving to Ambersville for Pa Charlie and Molly-Mae's wedding and our birthday celebration, meeting up with Mama and Daddy. Molly-Mae was aflutter with talk of all the treats she'd been baking: petit fours, tiramisu, a three-tiered cake. But that all seemed a lifetime away.

Tonight was *it*.

Every second that ticked us closer to the moonrise felt longer than normal, loaded and slow. Every movement I made, every breath I pulled in, carried a weight with it.

Tempest and I stayed clear of each other.

I kept touching the cuff on my wrist, just to check that it was still there.

With it being our last night here on the island, the carnival was less crowded than usual. When we ran out of work to do in the animal tent, Digger and I rode the Spaceship 3000 three times in a row. I screamed myself hoarse, and I tried to forget for a little while. Not that it worked.

The evening seemed to move along more quietly than usual. As though everyone—all the carnies, even the customers—were holding their collective breath. And maybe they didn't even know why.

There was something in the air that seemed poised, ready to explode.

I mean, the carnival still produced its usual noise. But after a while I noticed there was something strange in it, and that pricked at the back of my mind. At first, I thought it was just a horde of evening-time crickets chirping in the background, an even three-note, screechy rhythm.

As I was working with Molly-Mae, spinning the cotton candy, I started to become more and more conscious of it, as the sound deepened and filled out.

"You hear that?" I asked Molly-Mae.

She stopped what she was doing at the cash register. "Hear what?"

"That *ba-dum-clunk* noise."

We stood still and listened. Molly-Mae shook her head. "Tally, you have better ears than me. I don't hear anything like that."

"I need just a minute," I said, and I untied my apron and washed my hands. I stepped outside of the Candy Wagon, and I reveled in the cool air. The temperature had dropped considerably. It was just the right kind of weather for a storm, something big and hairy like in the jigsaw puzzles that Pa Charlie used to do with us. We'd put together a whole series of them one summer: a tornado, a hurricane, and even a tsunami.

No wonder there weren't many people out tonight.

Goose bumps rose on my arms, and I perked my ears to find where the noise was coming from. It thumped against my eardrums, reverberated into my teeth.

The noise grew, and the little baby hairs on the back of my neck lifted up. I turned toward the Iron Witch.

I took a few steps toward the ride, and I knew that was it. The Iron Witch, grinding and clanking, like it was working too hard.

I hurried closer.

The ancient Tilt-a-Whirl was silhouetted against the horizon. The blood-orange moon, too large, too imposing, in the storm-darkening sky. Menacing, powerful. Near.

The Flower Moon.

The wind kicked up and blew the flyaways around my face. And instantly, I knew. This was what we were waiting for. The disaster. I moved toward the Iron Witch.

It was going fast now, the cars spinning at their highest speeds in their elliptical orbits, looking as if they might crash, but barely missing each other. Car after car whizzed past the onlookers, creating a wind that blew back my hair, even from ten feet away.

"Fat Sam!" I yelled.

He was bent near the controls, pouring barf dust on a newly minted pile. "Sam!" I tried again, but he didn't look up.

It was then I noticed Digger, sitting cross-legged on the seashell-gravel of the midway, playing tug-of-war with a healthy looking Pork Chop. I called Digger's name, but he didn't answer. The music from the rides, the chug and clang of the engines, the yelping and laughing of the carnival-goers, all of that noise drowned out my voice.

Then, across the midway, near her numbers booth, I spotted Tempest. She stood ramrod straight, and she looked right toward me. She knew too.

In that moment, we both knew.

And I'm not going to lie. It sparked between us. Whatever we were creating in the air, it lit up blue and green between my sister and me, like a bolt of lightning, an electrical charge on the midway.

I froze for a second, feeling the *ba-dum-clunk* of the Iron Witch, knowing something was dead wrong.

Digger looked up from his lap, Pork Chop still focused on chewing a hole through the hem of his shirt.

Some decisions you don't make consciously.

I began to run. But it was like I was in a dream, moving through quicksand, slow and burdened.

And suddenly, the noise was more than a *ba-dum-clunk*. It was a clinking and clanking, a jangling of things that were coming apart, metal from metal, rust giving way. A screeching, creaking scream of a sound.

The music of the Iron Witch rose to a fever pitch. Its speed did the same. "Stop the ride!" I yelled to Fat Sam. I ran, as fast as I could. I pushed past people on the midway. "Stop the ride!"

And Fat Sam looked up. Thank God for small favors. "It's going to break off! One of the cars! You gotta stop it, Sam!"

He turned toward his control board, and I watched as he pulled the gearshift, yanking it to the full stop position. Suddenly I was next to him, and we were both looking up at the ride itself. It stuttered and hissed, the metal gears and mechanisms slowing. Something creaked and sputtered and, as if in slow motion, I watched one of the empty cars rock back and forth—thank the jelly donut that it was one of the empty ones—and then it came loose, tearing off its track. It flew through the air, like something from a cheap science-fiction movie.

And it headed right across the midway, toward Digger and Pork Chop. Digger threw his arms up, as if he could shield himself and protect the pup from the ton of screeching metal careening toward him at breakneck speed.

I moved before I decided to do so. But I was too far away. I couldn't get to him.

And then I heard Tempest. We can stop it.

And I knew she was right.

Together.

Fear shimmied its way down my neck. This wasn't us just messing around with metallic bugs. We were going to have to use the full force of our power.

Believe, Tally.

In that split second, that blip of time, I understood. What this was all about. All of this.

Every last thing.

Life.

It's as simple as this: Life is good; life is bad. Sometimes it's really good; sometimes it's really bad.

You can't always save the ones you love from being hurt.

But sometimes . . . sometimes when the moon is big and round and you're full of magic and you're extra brave, maybe you have a chance.

So I believed.

I closed my eyes, and I dug deep. I let that spark inside me take flight. I funneled my energy, let it spin and swirl, shuffle and spout from inside me, stronger than I'd ever dared. But I didn't just let it loose; I searched for Tempest's energy and found it.

Always there.

That's what Tempest was to me, the baseline of my life, my touchstone.

Inside me, that ever-present, live-wire thrum clicked into an easier rhythm, latching on to Tempest's, settling into something calm and right.

I focused my energy with hers, and together . . . it was like we stopped time. Suspended it. And just like those dragonflies and copper ants and butterflies, we moved the car.

It was a monstrous task. I broke out in a sweat, cold and full of terror. Adrenaline shot through my veins, and every muscle in my body tensed. But I held my energy, pushed when Tempest pulled. Pulled when she pushed. And we got ahold of the runaway car as it sailed straight for Digger. We couldn't move it much. But we moved it enough, just enough, mere inches from disaster, the gold-painted door handle skimming past, only a breath from the brim of Digger's baseball hat.

The air from the car, the motion of it, blew Digger back, his body pushed flat on the asphalt, Pork Chop curled into his arms. But that car landed with a screech and groan, sparks flying, only a foot or so away, throwing up shells and gravel. Missing Digger so very nearly, but missing him nonetheless. The car from the Iron Witch skidded and turned over itself. The metal hissed and bent, twisting and sparking, finally coming to a stop as I watched in awe.

Then I was running toward my friend. And in an instant, I was bent over him. "Digger!"

Tempest stood at my shoulder.

Digger sat up. "You know?" he said, his voice cracking. "Close only counts in horseshoes."

I let out a yelp of hysterical laughter, punching him in the shoulder. He lifted one free hand from Pork Chop and rubbed at the spot. "Ow, Tally."

I knelt on the ground and I threw my arms around him, darn near squashing Pork Chop, whose little tail wagged so hard it hit me in the eye and made it water. But I didn't let go of Digger's shoulders. If anything, I held him tighter to me, my face buried in his neck. "Digger," I said, and I kept saying it, so very relieved. "Digger."

And then I looked up, and there was Tempest hovering over us. I hesitated, unsure of the risk, but then I grabbed my sister. I pulled her into the hug too, all three of us collapsing in a heap. And I was fighting tears, and there was a pressure in my throat, and I couldn't seem to say anything, and I couldn't get a breath.

Digger—I wanted to tell him. Tempest—I needed to tell her. Did they know? Did they have any idea what they meant to me? The words were too big in my throat, choking me, the feelings too buoyant in my heart, like I could float away.

"Girls!"

It was Mama's voice, and Tempest and I turned around to see our mama and daddy coming from the direction of the Candy Wagon. Mama running, Daddy on her heels.

"Girls!" she yelled again. "What's happened?"

The Iron Witch's car took that as its cue to burst into half-hearted flames.

"Mom," Tempest yelped.

"Girls!" she said a third time, and Tempest and I tried to get out some explanation, but Mama wasn't listening. She was pulling us away from the car, and then in for hugs. Daddy joined her, and he held up my wrist cuff. They both talked at once. Didn't we know we were supposed to call them if anything weird happened? Why hadn't we listened to them?

Didn't we realize how precious we were to them?

What had we been thinking?

Did we like giving them gray hair?

Were we hurt?

Was there a doctor in town?

Was Digger okay?

Tempest and I answered the questions, took the lectures. Endured the hugs.

Together.

We were together.

Butter on toast. Sea to shore. Both sides of the moon.

We were sisters again.

But then Mama stiffened in my arms. And she pulled away. She gasped with her whole body. "Grania?"

22

"Don't come any closer!" Aunt Grania yelled as she stepped out from behind the port-o-johns, followed by Molly-Mae and Licorice. "Genevieve!" Aunt Grania cried, and her voice broke. She put her hand over her mouth, a sob racking her shoulders.

"Wait! It's okay," Tempest said to Mama. "I've been working on something." Tempest stuck her hand into one of the pockets of her cargo shorts.

"Girls!" Mama said again, and she was crying now. Surely we had scared the bejesus out of her with what she'd just seen. And now this! Aunt Grania here.

How many years had it been for them?

Tempest opened her fist, and I expected a bracelet, of course. But with Tempest, you just couldn't assume anything.

What she handed to Mama was the most delicate gold chain I'd ever seen, with a large silver locket dangling from it, decorated with tiny filigree flowers and geometric shapes. Tempest popped it open to show Mama, and instead of a clock or a photo of a loved one, there was some kind of a tiny, complicated mechanism inside. No dials. No face of any sort, just a mess of gears on one side, and a shiny, flat, metallic surface on the other.

"A magnet, magnified," Tempest said, as if this explained everything.

I nodded, and Mama took the chain from her, let it dangle from her hand. "What . . .?"

"Put it on," Tempest told her.

"When you called and told us to come today, you said Grania was gone," Mama said.

"I lied."

"Tempest!" Mama gasped.

"I needed you to come today, so that we could test this. And I know it's reckless, but it's too important—"

"Girls," Mama said again. I could tell she was trying to admonish us, to sound stern and angry, but the relief in her voice won out. I pulled her into a hug.

"We're okay, Mama. We're okay." I took the locket from her hand and I unlatched it. "Is it going to be enough?" I asked Tempest.

"I don't know, Tally."

"We have to try," I said. And that right there was another example of the real magic in this world: finding it inside yourself to be brave.

Mama pulled me into another hug then, before we had a chance to explain anything more. She grabbed Tempest too, and we all stood there, hugging and crying. "You girls! You're foolish. You should be punished. This is—"

"I know, Mama," I said, and I backed away from the hug. I put the necklace over her head, and I watched her tear-stricken face freeze as she registered something, some change. Was it the same feeling between Tempest and me when I slid on the cuff?

Did she understand?

But before I could open my mouth to explain, before I could do anything more, Digger was pulling a hesitant Aunt Grania by the hand toward Mama.

The Greenly sisters stood a few yards apart. They took tentative steps toward each other.

Tempest explained, "Aunt Grania said what you two have, it isn't as powerful as ours. Maybe the necklace—"

But then it didn't matter, because Mama and Aunt Grania were in each other's arms, and they were bawling. The whole place went nuts. Pa Charlie and Daddy, Fat Sam and Molly-Mae, everyone. Suddenly, Digger was hugging me, and I was hugging him back.

This was magic. Right here. The real kind.

And, wouldn't you know it? Digger wrapped an arm around my shoulders, and I leaned into it. He smelled like sweat and I didn't mind, and I squeezed his bird-bone ribs a little tighter, and I cried.

Me, tough Tally Jo Trimble, cried in front of everyone. Tears of relief. And hope—I guess there was some of that too.

And there was this thought. Well, maybe it was more than a thought; it was a feeling, a premonition, a knowing. We were powerful. Tempest and me. And that was a good thing.

We could do anything.

23

We hadn't beaten this thing for good—I knew that. But with the cuff and with the necklace, we'd reversed the polarity. We'd done enough for right now, anyway.

And maybe it wouldn't always be so easy, but that night, we danced our copper bugs for everyone, to the tune of Fat Sam's banjo. We watched as Mama and Aunt Grania linked hands, their heads bent together, deep in conversation, looking so much like the girls in our red-framed silhouette garland.

We sang country songs and roasted marshmallows. We heated Molly-Mae's apple pocket-pies over the fire, and we celebrated. Mama and Daddy asked us a thousand and one questions about what we figured out, barely any of which we could truly answer. But in the end, they chose to believe in what we had done.

To believe in our magic.

And now, back in our little pod, it was just us.

TallyandTempest. No spaces. Like it used to be.

No, that wasn't right. We were better than that.

We were Tally and Tempest. Fierce and brave and power-ful on our own. And together.

We were new, evolved.

My sister and I sat on the floor of our pod, cross-legged, knee to knee, even though we were on the road. And being in the pod while Pa Charlie was driving was technically illegal, but Pa Charlie overlooked it tonight, with all the happiness going on.

Tempest and I were going through a heap of pictures Aunt Grania had given us. They were of Mama and her when they were younger, but there were pictures of us too, through the years, a chronicle of the time she had missed with us. The years Mama had lived without her sister. We were too awake to sleep. "We're thirteen tonight exactly at 11:47," I said.

"Can you believe it?"

I played with the cuff on my wrist. "No."

Tempest asked, "Do you really think Mama and Aunt Grania will take over Peachtree, like they were saying tonight? When Pa retires?"

"I doubt Pa Charlie will ever leave the carnival."

"That's true. But now Aunt Grania and Mama don't have to, either." Tempest smiled so wide.

"We could travel every summer with them," I said. "We could really think up some cool stuff. Serious magic shows." And I shot her a mental picture of what I was thinking: Snowflakes. Real, icy snowflakes falling inside a large, silver tent, delighting a bewildered crowd. Constellations lighting up the ceiling, a large Flower Moon sitting on the makeshift horizon of the tent walls. I didn't know how we'd do it exactly, but I knew better than to question it.

Tempest flashed me an image right back. It was of Digger walking into that silver tent and sweeping me up in a sloppy, movie star–style kiss.

"Tempest Jean!" I yelped, and I stood up and grabbed the nearest thing, which happened to be a stuffed alligator, and I threw it at her as hard as I could. But Pa Charlie always warned us about standing in the pod while traveling, and the gods of traffic were not kind to me at that moment. Pa Charlie hit the brakes, and I went flying into the window right between our beds. I felt a thump and heard a crack as my elbow hit the windowsill, and next thing I knew I was sitting on my rump on the floor, blood dripping down my arm.

"Holy cow," Tempest said. "You okay?"

I touched my elbow, looked at my fingers and saw the blood there. Tempest handed me a tissue. We jerked forward and accelerated at a steady pace. I looked at the window, and it didn't seem cracked. But then I noticed that only half of the lady bug suncatcher still hung there. The other half was on the floor at my feet. I picked that one up, and Tempest took it from me, tossing it into her box of junk.

I dabbed my elbow with the tissue. "You okay?" she asked again.

"I'm fine."

"Does it hurt?"

"Nah," I said.

"You're lying."

"Yeah." I laughed.

She smiled back, and then we fell into a hug. It was more than a hug though; it was a reunion, and I stifled a little sob.

It felt real good to hug Tempest.

Tempest grabbed something from the nightstand drawer then, and I saw it was her yearbook. "Here," she said. "Look at what Bradley wrote."

She flipped it open and handed it over to me. That day, our last day at school, it seemed like forever ago. Tempest pointed to a small handwritten note in red ink: YOU'RE STUPID.

I smiled in spite of myself. I giggled, and when I looked up at Tempest I saw that she was grinning too. Then we both laughed. "You're stupid," I said, all matter-of-factly, sending us into a new fit of laughter. I had tears in my eyes when I finally settled down.

"Okay," I said. "I admit it. Maybe he's not worth the effort."

"Sometimes I can handle myself."

"I know you can."

"It's been hard . . . to grow up, I think. I could've spent my whole life just being your shadow."

"You're so much more than that, Tempest."

"I know." She leaned over and pulled something out of her pillowcase. "Happy birthday," she told me. "Just a bit early."

I took the small envelope from her hand. "I got you something too, from the shell shop by the pier, but it's wrapped and in Pa's trailer . . ."

Tempest shook her head. "Just open it."

I opened the cream-colored envelope, and in there was a yellow index card, folded in half. And before I had unfolded it, I knew what it was. The nail polish had chipped and cracked over the years, but it was the same. "Our fingerprints."

"We can be different. But we're still together. We'll always be together."

"Tempest, that's all I need. Because you're you, and I love you. I'm sorry if I ever made you think you had to be something else. I'm sorry I was ever embarrassed by your pigtails."

"They keep the flyaways away from your face much better than a ponytail."

I considered this. "I suppose that's true."

Tempest smiled then, but she didn't meet my eyes. Whatever she was about to say, I could see it was hard for her. "I know I'm not the easiest to have around at school. I don't make friends easily, like you do, and I'm always shy and . . . you know."

"Tempest, no. I tried to blame you for so long, for us growing apart. But it was both of us, I think. I was just the one being mean about it."

"We can grow apart in some ways, but we'll still always be us. Together in the way that matters."

I nodded. "I was a wreck, thinking we would have to split up like Mama and Aunt Grania. I could never, ever want that."

Tempest nodded. "We are strong. Together and alone."

"Thank you," I said, folding the fingerprint paper, and setting it on my pillow. "Hey, Tempest?"

"Yeah?"

"Is Ambersville the place where we set up right next to that milkweed field?"

"Yeah, I think so," she answered. "Right near the church. Just think of it, Tally. Mama and Aunt Grania will both get to be there for Pa Charlie's wedding."

"Yeah," I said, smiling. We had done that. Made that possible.

Tempest leaned over and reached into a drawer in the nightstand. She worked at opening a Band-Aid for my elbow.

I knew that tomorrow I would let this card, with our tiny fingerprints on it, blow away in that milkweed field, just like the image from my dream so many weeks ago. I didn't need to be reminded that Tempest and I were different, or that we were the same. We were both and neither.

Some things are bigger than words or paper or fingerprints. Some things need no reminders.

Tempest slapped a Band-Aid onto my arm, and then we both lay down in our beds.

I fingered my copper cuff and listened to Tempest's breathing, and I let mine match hers. And I was me again. A new me. A growing-up me, evolving, changing.

"I was so sure this was going to be our last summer together," Tempest said sleepily. "I'm so glad it's not."

"I know," I said, turning on my side. And there was my sister, across from me, her silhouette outlined by moonlight. "It could've been the worst summer ever. It could've been the end."

"But it's not. It's definitely not," Tempest agreed.

And I knew, back in the recesses of my brain, that this summer would be the time I would forever look back on as *the* summer. The best summer. The one to compare all others to.

The summer my sister and I learned how to grow up, on our own terms.

The summer we learned what to pull close to our hearts, what was worth fighting for.

The summer we bested the moon.

Acknowledgments

Heartfelt gratitude goes out to my editor extraordinaire, Rachel Stark, for seeing a spark in Tally and Tempest, and working tirelessly to forge this book into a truly special story. Thank you to Caryn Wiseman, my agent and friend, for believing in my writing for so many years now. Thank you to Manuel Šumberac and Sammy Yuen for this enchanting, bittersweet cover, and to Joshua Barnaby, Ming Liu, Jenn Chan, Sarah Dean, Alison Weiss, Diane Wood, Bethany Bryan, Emma Dubin, and everyone at Sky Pony Press for their unwavering support of *Flower Moon*. It means the world to me.

And, of course, thank you to my dear readers. For you, I have a special secret. Like Tally Jo Trimble, if you look inside yourself, deep down, in that most secret corner of your heart, you'll find that you've got something too. Call it magic, call it power, call it whatever you like. It's yours, and know this: I believe in you.